A Home for
Shimmer
Cathy Hopkins

A Home for Shimmer

Cathy Hopkins

SIMON AND SCHUSTER

First published in Great Britain in 2015 by Simon and Schuster UK Ltd
A CBS COMPANY

3 5 7 9 10 8 6 4 2

Simon & Schuster UK Ltd
1st Floor, 222 Gray's Inn Road
London
WC1X 8HB

www.simonandschuster.co.uk

Simon & Schuster Australia, Sydney
Simon & Schuster India, New Delhi

A CIP catalogue record for this book
is available from the British Library.

PB ISBN: 978-1-47111-793-0
EBOOK ISBN: 978-1-47111-794-7

Printed and bound by CPI Group (UK) Ltd, Croydon, CR0 4YY

For Amy Smith and her real-life dog, Shimmer

Chapter One

Newbie Time

'It will be fine, honey. You'll make friends before you know it. Text me later, OK?' said Mum as I got out of the car into the cold, wet February day.

I shut the door and waved goodbye to her from the pavement. I turned and looked at the pebbledash buildings spread out in front of me, into which hundreds of pupils were swarming like bees into hives. Like me, they were dressed in a grey uniform with white shirt – but unlike me, they all knew each other. I felt terrified. *Easy for Mum to say it will be fine*, I thought as she drove off, leaving me to face the unknown. I'd been dreading this day for weeks. I'd be the new girl at a school with over a thousand pupils in Somerset. I'd never felt so alone in all my life. Mum didn't understand. I'd be going into Year Seven halfway through the winter term. Everyone would already have their friends sorted, from the start of the school year in September.

Groups of girls with their arms linked, chatting away, passed me by. One gave me a brief, curious look, then carried on walking. Others called to each other; one threw a book that caught her mate on the back of the head. I knew I had to go in but I felt stuck to the spot, as if my feet had grown roots. The bell went and everyone speeded up. I took a deep breath. *I can do this*, I told myself. *I'm not scared.* But I was. I made myself remember the pep talk given by Mum and Dad this morning over breakfast. 'A new chapter. Be brave. Yadah yadah,' they'd said, and they were right. The move from city life in Bristol to the countryside village of Compton Truit was a big change for all of us. I wanted to be strong. I wanted to walk in with my head high, not skulk in like a scaredy cat.

What would Lady Gaga do if she was about to start a new school? I asked myself.

She'd strut right in with mad hair and a rubber chicken hat on her head. The answer came back from my inner Lady G. *Head high. Get in there, girl.*

I was about to assume Lady Gaga attitude (without the chicken hat, obv) and join the moving crowd when I noticed a girl had come to stand next to me.

Her shoulder-length hair was the colour of dark rubies and her eyes were jade green. With my mousey-brown hair pulled back from my face in a ponytail and my normal, hazel-coloured eyes, I felt pale and boring next to her.

'You new?' she said.

I nodded.

'Thought so,' she said. 'Me too. Shall we do a runner?'

I liked her immediately. She had an open, friendly face and her eyes were full of mischief.

I laughed. 'That's *exactly* what I feel like doing.'

She linked her arm through mine. 'Well now there's two of us,' she said, 'so it won't be so bad. My name's Caitlin O'Neill.'

'I'm Amy,' I said. 'Amy Westall.'

She looked at the school and, just as I had a moment earlier, she took a deep breath. 'We'll get soaked if we stay here much longer, so come on, Amy Westall, let's do it. Now, tell me all about yourself …' she said as we marched in, arms linked, like the best of old friends.

'So what brings you to this part of the world?' asked Caitlin at lunch, when we'd found two empty seats in the dining room. Every table was full of girls eating, talking, laughing, making loads of noise. It was the first chance we'd had to talk properly because as soon as we'd got inside the school we'd been grabbed by a tall skinny lady with blonde frizzy hair and watery blue eyes. She turned out to be our class teacher, Mrs Lawson, and she escorted Caitlin and me round the school, showing us where we had to be for classes, where the cloakrooms and the dining room were. Caitlin kept a few steps behind her and mimicked the way she walked (briskly with stiff arms and legs) and mouthed the words that she was saying as though Caitlin was a ventriloquist and Mrs Lawson was her dummy. I would never dare do something like that, but it didn't stop me cracking up at Caitlin, then having to pretend I was having a coughing fit. After the tour, we went in to meet our new classmates – and Caitlin was right, it wasn't as bad as I'd imagined. Now that I had a friend who seemed like she was going to be a laugh, my shyness and anxiety about meeting so many evaporated.

'Long story,' I replied, as I got out my cheese and tomato sandwich and an apple. 'Short version is that my parents have gone insane—'

'Mine too,' interrupted Caitlin. 'Actually not just recently, they've always been bonkers.'

'Mine too, but it got worse this year.'

4

'What happened?' asked Caitlin through a mouthful of crisps.

'They went to Glastonbury—'

'The music festival?'

I nodded. 'That part wasn't so bad, but while they were there, they went to a workshop run by an old friend of my dad's. They were at school and uni together, then Dad became a vet—'

'Your dad's a vet? Cool. I *love* animals, especially cats. Our old cat, Smokey, died before we moved. I blubbed for weeks. Sorry. I'm always interrupting people. Go on. Your dad's old mate?'

'Yeah. He went to India to find himself—'

'He should have just looked the mirror then he'd have gone: "Oh, there I am. I've found myself."'

'I *so* wished he'd stayed in India,' I laughed, 'but he didn't. He came back and set himself up as a New Age guru. We used to laugh about it. "Uncle Robin. Haha. What a nutter." Then he invited Mum and Dad to go to Glastonbury, to stay in his posh yurt, and attend his "find yourself" workshop for free. At first Mum and Dad didn't want to go, but seeing as they'd never been to a festival, they thought why not? A weekend in the country, some good music and a few of Robin's boring lectures thrown in. "We're not old yet," they said. And off they went with their

5

camping gear and wellies like a pair of old hippies. *So* embarrassing.'

'Didn't they take you?'

'No, they packed me off to my aunt's house. They weren't the same when they came back. Dad especially. He said he wanted to change his life. That "life isn't a rehearsal and we all have to make the most of the time we've got".'

'Unbe*liev*able,' said Caitlin. 'Something similar happened to my dad. He used to be a teacher. We lived in Swindon and he taught geography. Everything changed for him when Grandad died. After that, Dad was different. He said, and I quote, "Life is too short to waste and I want to do something I feel passionate about," so he packed in his job and we moved down here.'

'Mid–life crisis,' I said.

Caitlin nodded. 'Exactly. Must be their hormones.'

We both sighed and looked out of the window for a moment.

'So what does your dad do now?' I asked.

'Organic farming. He's got this idea about growing vegetables. He's actually a lot happier, but I don't think courgettes earn him as much money as his last job. He's always going on about "following his heart" though.'

'I don't believe it! That's *exactly* what Dad said when

6

he came back from Glastonbury. Those very words. "We have to follow our hearts." *He* packed his job in too.'

'What? Isn't he a vet any more?'

'Well yes, but it's different here. Where we lived before, it was posh poodles and pedigree cats, that sort of thing. Here, he's hoping to work with all sorts of animals but the practice isn't open yet because—'

'What town did you live in?'

Wow – Caitlin really did like interrupting.

'Bristol. But Dad was brought up in a tiny village in Somerset and he wanted to get back to his roots.'

'And all this happened after Glastonbury?'

I nodded. 'It all happened so fast. Mum and Dad put our house on the market and it sold really quickly, then they saw a place down here and suddenly, as if someone waved a magic wand, abracadabra, here we are. Old life gone, new life started. Josh, my brother, and I—'

'You have a brother?'

I nodded.

'How old?'

'Thirteen.'

'Handsome?' Caitlin asked with a cheeky grin.

I nodded. *Here we go again*, I thought. Girls were falling over themselves to get close to Josh recently. 'He doesn't know it though. He only likes animals and designing stuff on his computer. He's not interested in girls.'

'He hasn't met *me*,' said Caitlin.

I laughed. 'What about your mum?' I asked.

'She's a nurse,' said Caitlin. 'Dad moved here first, the summer before last. He came to get things set up and start planting the vegetables, and then when Mum got a job at the local hospital last month, we all came too. That's Mum, me and my two younger brothers. What about your mum?'

'She used to work as a receptionist for a dentist. She's not sure what she's going to do down here yet. She wasn't as keen as Dad to move, but he talked her into it.'

Caitlin grinned. 'Did he talk her into following her heart too?'

I nodded.

'Imagine,' Caitlin continued, 'if your heart jumped out of your body, out of your chest, *budoink*, *splat*, on to the pavement and you literally had to follow it as it splat, splat, splatted down the road.'

'Ew! You've been watching too many horror films.'

Caitlin nodded. 'My brothers love them. We're not supposed to watch them, but whenever Mum or Dad leave the room, over the channel goes into spook or zombie land. What about you? Did you want to move?'

I sighed. 'No. Nobody asked about *my* heart,' I said. 'If they had, they'd have heard it saying "Nooooo," very loudly.'

Caitlin nodded. 'Me too. I was so freaked out about leaving my old friends. But nobody listens to me in our house.' She looked around the packed room. I thought again how glad I was to have met with Caitlin. It would have been awful sitting here on my own like a loner. 'I reckon we can either sink or swim here, Amy Westall,' Caitlin continued. 'We can be miserable for the rest of our lives, or make the most of it.'

I liked her attitude. 'Let's swim!' I said.

We both mimed front crawl at the same time and then burst out laughing. We were completely in sync already. Our air swimming caused a few funny looks from people nearby, but I didn't care. For me, it sealed the deal. My new friend was super fun and didn't care what people thought of her.

'Great,' said Caitlin. 'We can't change the fact we're here. Maybe it won't be so bad and maybe we'll get to follow *our* hearts when we're older. I want to be an actress. What about you?'

'Not sure yet. Maybe artist. Maybe writer. I like making up stories.'

'Cooool,' said Caitlin. 'Maybe you can write me a part and we can both be famous.'

By the time we left school that day, we'd already swapped phone numbers and email addresses and had arranged to meet at each other's houses. Life in Compton Truit was looking up already.

Chapter Two

Sad Cat, Stray Cat

'Mum, it's freezing,' I called down the stairs, 'can't you put the heating on?'

'It is on. Put another layer on,' Mum called back. All week she'd been saying, 'Put another jumper on ... put another pair of socks on ...' It's because the heating system here is prehistoric and the boiler gurgles, which is spooky late at night. I thanked God my old friends in Bristol couldn't see me sitting here on a Saturday morning with a woolly hat on *indoors*. I caught a glimpse of myself in the mirror on my wardrobe. A girl with long hair wearing a green bobble hat stared back. I tried pulling the hat over to one side to make it look more stylish but it looked even madder. I didn't care. It was cold.

Caitlin was coming over later so I got out my diary while I was waiting for her.

Dear Diary

I have landed on the moon. Might as well be, as it's a million miles away from life as I know it.

Nearest shops: over half a mile away. Nightmare.

School: Some snooty girls, some boring teachers, but mostly OK and not as bad as I thought it would be. Love the art teacher, Mrs Rendall, which is good because art is one of my favourite subjects. She's mad (in a nice way), très stylish, and made me feel very welcome. She loves interior design and got us looking at loads of ideas for decorating houses, which I can pass on to Mum.

New house: not so new. Where we live is called Silverbrook Farm and it was built in the 1800s. It's a draughty farmhouse that has been extended over the years. It has low beams in every room which Dad keeps banging his head on. If he carries on this way, he is going to get concussion. I bet the house is haunted. We don't even have a satellite dish because we are in the middle of NOWHERE surrounded by fields, trees, sheep and barns that are falling down. Also empty stables that are full of cobwebs and stink of horse poo, and there's a barn at the end which is run as a tea shop by Mrs Watson, who is the widow of the vet who was here before Dad took over. Mr Watson died last year, which is why his veterinary practice came up for sale. I wonder if he's haunting the place. Perhaps it's not the boiler that's making a noise in the middle of the night, but his ghost. Wooooooooo. Agh! I'm scaring myself. I say tea shop, but it's basically a big shed with a couple of rickety old tables and chairs and a counter with a large tea urn for the people who come by with their animals and want a drink while they wait. I think Dad would prefer not to have to provide tea as part of his services but he's a real softie and Mrs Watson's been doing it for years. 'Gives her a reason to get out of the house in the morning and see people,' Dad says. I think he's a bit scared of her. She's not very friendly and is always telling Dad how her husband used to do things.

My new bedroom: paint is peeling off the ceiling. It is in every room. There's a damp patch in the corner and the wallpaper looks like it was put up about a hundred years ago. It was probably was. Pale green with little pink roses on it. So last century. The floorboards creak (also spooky at night). Plus the whole house has a musty smell. Yuck. Mum says it's a new room spray called Eau de Damp. She thinks she is being funny.

Dad and Josh love it here. They are bonkers. I can tell Mum still has reservations. She says she has *found the locals unwelcoming but she is being Cheery Mum which is Very Annoying. I'm not sure I like it here either. I miss my old life despite having met Caitlin. In Bristol, I knew loads of people.*

I closed my diary and texted Natalia, my best friend back in Bristol. *Help! I'm in the middle of Nowhereland,* I wrote.

Her reply pinged through a minute later. *I'd swap with u any day. Ur so lucky.*

I knew she wouldn't be sympathetic. She'd always wanted to live in the country. When I first got to Silverbrook, she insisted that I Skype her then carry my laptop around and show her exactly where we were. She loved it, saying it looked romantic.

I texted back. *Knickers to you.*

Underpants to you, she texted back. *Exploding ones.*

Natalia and I can have deep and meaningful conversations that go on like that for hours. We pride ourselves on them. Mum said it's juvenile to text such silly messages to your friend. She can talk. She says 'Oh, poo!' when she's fed up – and if that's not juvenile, I don't know what is.

I put the phone aside and got up to look out of the window. Caitlin was coming to hang out. I did explain to her that hang out was all we could do because there

14

is nothing to do here apart from look at trees or go New Age mad and hug them.

'That's cool,' she'd said, but I got the feeling that she was as much a townie as I was.

As I stared at the grey skies and mist outside, Ginger, our cat, leaped up on to the windowsill and sat looking out longingly. 'Countryside, lots of it to see,' I said to him, 'and lots and lots of rain.' There were views from every window and some days, you could see for miles over fields to hills in the far distance. But for the last week, all I had seen was drizzle.

Ginger's the family cat, but everyone knows that he's really Josh's. Ginger loves my brother and follows him around the house like a dog would. He sleeps in his bed, sometimes actually on Josh's head. Mum wasn't too happy about him being in Josh's room most of the time, but when she told Josh to close his door at night, Ginger howled the place down, clawed at the door and kept us all awake so Mum relented. He's a funny cat. We think he imagines that he's from royal blood because he always likes to sit above the rest of us if he can – on a shelf or top of cupboard – and look down on us as if we are his loyal servants – which we are – running about opening doors for him when he cries, giving him food or water when he goes to his food bowl. He's been stuck in the house for over three weeks now, since we arrived, and he's not happy about it but Dad said under no circumstances were we to allow him out, no matter how much he paws at the window or cries, or he might run away from our new house. We don't want to lose him, but he's dying to get out there and start exploring. I asked if I could have a pet of my own but Mum said no. I've a good mind to write to the prime minister and let him know that I am being ignored in this family on every level.

'I know, Ginger,' I said as I stroked his head. '*So* unfair.'

He butted my hand with his head in reply.

I felt so lonely when we first arrived in Compton Truit. I even cried myself to sleep the first few nights. I'm not usually a cry baby but I missed Natalia and I'd been brought to this bleak cold place where the only sign of life outside is chickens. Dad went and bought those last week. 'This is just the beginning,' he said and looked at me as if he expected me to do a dance of joy. Over chickens. *I know.* Mum wasn't too pleased either. She often gets cross with Dad and says that he has his head in the clouds. She's right. He does live in his own world. Mum's always saying, 'Earth to Richie, Earth to Richie …' It seems like he lives in a happy world though. He looks like an absent-minded professor, with his messy dark hair and glasses, and he doesn't care about clothes at all. He often wears odd socks or puts his jumper on inside out. He especially annoys Mum when he does his tuneless humming. It's never a song you can recognise. I can tell how Mum is feeling about Dad by the way she comments on it. If she's in a good mood and Dad comes in going, 'Lala, mnn, nn,' she will say in a normal tone of voice, 'Richie – humming.' If she's in a bad mood, she will say, 'Richie!' then add in a sharp voice, '*Humming.*' He takes notice to begin with, then forgets he's doing it and wanders off again going, 'Hmm, nmm, hmm, nmm.' I don't mind it, plus it lets me know when he's coming, which isn't a bad thing when I'm reading under the covers past my bedtime. Mum and Dad are an unlikely pair; opposites really. She's small, blonde and neat and used to dress in smart clothes when we lived in Bristol, though she's taken to wearing fleeces, jeans and wellies since we got here. With all the mud outside, we have no choice. She used to take a lot of pride in her appearance and liked the getting-dressed-up part of her job. I wonder if she misses it.

Josh shares Dad's enthusiasm about the move. He's loved it here from the start. He loves the outdoors whatever the weather, unlike me who is happier inside snuggled up with a book or watching TV. Out of the window, I could see him and Dad strutting around in the land to the right of the house. Both were oblivious to the rain. All they talked about now was boring stuff like fencing or what they could do with the stables. I suggested knocking them down and building a leisure park and they both laughed as if I was joking. I wasn't. Mum's not been around either, she's been up and down to the village buying paint or buying furniture online, busy and happy to have a project.

'It's just you and me, Ginger.'

'Meow,' he replied and put his paw up to the window again.

I could see a car coming up the lane. I don't know what kind because I'm not into cars apart from what colour they are. This was a green one. It drove into the yard and stopped. Caitlin got out of the passenger side and looked up at the house. She was dressed in jeans, a red quilted jacket over a navy jumper with silver hearts on it, a grey knitted scarf and grey Converse. She looked older and very cool. I whipped off my hat before she saw me then raced down the stairs to find her already chatting away to Dad and Josh.

A man with a beard and tousled red hair got out of the car. Caitlin introduced him as her dad.

He gestured at the house and land with his arms. 'Amazing place you got here,' he said to my dad. 'Great position.' They seemed to hit it off immediately and soon Dad was showing him around. He looked nothing like a geography teacher, more like a country and western singer in jeans, a red checked shirt and leather jacket.

'So you're at Amy's school?' Josh asked Caitlin. I was pleased that he'd asked her but I knew that he was being polite rather than actually interested. Mum had drilled it into us both to make conversation with visitors and not act, as she put it, 'like gormless idiots who don't have a tongue in their heads'. As if. Mum can be Very Insulting as well as Annoying and Strict.

Caitlin nodded, put her head to one side and looked at him coyly. 'Amy told me she had a handsome brother,' she said.

Josh looked embarrassed by her attention. He looked around like he wanted to get away, which made Caitlin laugh, which made Josh even *more* embarrassed.

'I so did not,' I said. 'I said I had a brother. End of.'

Caitlin punched my arm playfully. 'Just joshing,' she said. 'Nice to meet you, Josh.'

'You too,' said Josh but he was already backing away and looking in Dad's direction. 'Er … think I'll go and join … over there.' And off he stumbled.

'He's quite shy really,' I said when he'd gone. 'And I told you he wasn't into girls.'

Caitlin looked after him. 'Give me time,' she said, then continued in a strange accent, 'no-von can resist ze charms of la belle femme Madame Caitlin O'Neill.'

'I wouldn't bother. He's boring really, just into animals, being outdoors and computer games,' I said.

Caitlin looked over in the direction that Josh'd gone. 'Didn't look boring to me,' she said, then sighed longingly, a bit like Ginger had earlier when he'd looked outside.

'So give me the grand tour,' she said when we saw that Josh had caught up with our dads.

'Where do you want to start – in or out?' I asked.

'In,' said Caitlin. 'And pretend you're an estate agent and I'm looking to buy.'

I laughed. 'You're the one who wants to be an actress, not me.'

'All good practice,' said Caitlin. 'I am ze very rich foreign lady who is looking to invest her money. You want to be a writer, make up a story.'

'OK, Madame Belle Femme, step this way,' I said as I led her through the hall into the kitchen. 'Follow me. Inside, the décor is shabby chic … with plenty of shab but not much chic. Some estate agents might say "in need of modernisation". I'd say, the place is falling down and I don't think it's been redecorated in a hundred years. Note the original flagstone flooring and how it has been worn away by the feet of those gone before us. The house has four bedrooms upstairs and has built-in air conditioning because there are draughts everywhere, ensuring a flow of cold air at all times of the day, whether you like it or not. And in here, a typical farmhouse style kitchen,' I pointed above at the dark wooden beams, 'the beams date back to the days of our ancestors and the damp patches by the window give the place an authentic sense of history.'

'*Merveilleux*,' said Caitlin. 'Or, as you say in English – fantabulous.'

'And if you follow me, we have a cosy living room through here. The stone fireplace you can see and the heavy velvet drapes came with the house.'

Caitlin wrinkled her nose. 'And vot is dat smell?'

'Eau de Peat. From the fire. Dad builds a real fire most nights because the house is freezing.'

'*Oui, je comprends*. It is – how you say? – quaint?'

'No. We don't say "quaint", we say "paint" – and the whole house needs loads, as well as a whole refurb from top to toe,' I said.

'I like it,' said Caitlin. 'It's got a lot of oldie-worldie character.'

I showed Caitlin upstairs and she followed me around commenting here and there as we went from room to room. 'And vot are the neighbours like?' she asked in her unidentifiable foreign accent that kept going from Russian to Indian.

'Ah, the neighbours. They cluck a lot and lay eggs, apart from that, they're no trouble,' I said as we went downstairs and I led her outside to the side of the house to the extension that served as Dad's clinic.

Caitlin let out a big puff of air. 'Look, it's so cold I can see my breath.'

'I know. I don't remember it ever being this cold in Bristol,' I said.

'Is that why the previous owner sold up – too cold for him?'

'No … um … he died – which is why the practice came up for sale. Dad used to work in a centre where there were three vets but here, it's just him.' We peeked in the windows of the clinic but there was nothing much to see – Dad's office, a small waiting area with loads of posters on the wall and to the back, a room where he treated the animals. Like the house, it was run-down-looking, in need of decorating and some new furniture.

'He hasn't had a lot of work since he got here,' I said. 'Mrs Watson told him that's because he's an outsider. She said it will take time to earn the locals' trust, and that her husband was born and went to school here so everyone knew him.'

'She doesn't sound very friendly,' said Caitlin. 'Though my dad's found the same, I think. He said it takes a while for people here to let you in and that starting a new business takes time.'

In the fields in the distance, we could see our dads chatting away. Josh was still with them. 'Maybe our dads can be friends.'

Caitlin turned to look. 'Looks like they are already. Cool.'

'They're doing the fence pointing dance,' I said as we watched them take turns in pointing at things. 'Dad and Josh are always doing it these days. One points, one turns, another points.'

Caitlin made up a version of the dance. Point, turn, point – then she added a knee bend, which of course I copied. 'Looks like they're getting on though,' she said. 'So where to next, Mrs Estate Agent?'

'Er … next I'll show you the holiday homes,' I said and led Caitlin towards the stables.

Caitlin looked impressed. 'Seriously? You have holiday homes?'

I laughed. 'We do, mainly for small insects. Wait till you see them. Holiday homes for mice and spiders.'

Caitlin pulled back. 'Uck. Spiders. I don't do spiders.'

I went close to her and made my fingers walk up lightly up her arm and her neck. She shrieked and ran off. 'Madame Belle Femme doesn't like creepy-crawlies.'

I laughed. 'There's a sort of tea shop in one of the barns. Want to look? Mrs Watson comes and opens it up on weekdays. She lives in a cottage at the end of the lane now but still sees this place as her territory.'

'Only if there are no spiders,' she replied.

'No. Only bats in there.'

Caitlin pulled back again. I could see she was going to be easy to wind up. When she realised I was joking, she started to mock strangle me. 'You are ze crazee estate agent. I will have to keel you because I am not really a buyer, I am ze deadly assassin.'

I freed myself from her and began to run towards the front of the house with Caitlin chasing and doing karate chops after me. Both of us stopped because we could see a battered car (red) coming up the lane from the main road. It drew up outside the front door and an anxious-looking white-haired old lady carrying a cat basket got out.

I went over to her. 'Can I help you?' I asked.

The lady looked down at the basket. 'I'm Mrs Edwards from down the road. You can call me Lily. I've this cat here.'

'Oh,' I said. 'Have you come for my dad? He's the

vet. I'm afraid his clinic is closed this morning but he'll be open again on Monday.'

While we were talking, Caitlin knelt down to look at the cat. It was black with a white bib and had enormous gold eyes. 'Hello puss,' she said as the cat poked a paw through the wire of the basket's door. The cat meowed in response to Caitlin. 'Oh I think it's trying to talk to me. What's its name?'

The cat meowed again, which made Caitlin laugh. 'It's trying to tell me its name. Is it a girl or a boy?'

Dad, Mr O'Neill and Josh appeared round the corner and came over to see what was happening.

Lily shrugged. 'I don't know. Don't know if it's a he or a she or what its name is. Just I can't look after it. I know that. It came to my back door and won't go away, but I have cats, see. I got three of my own. Can't have no more. I was told that this is an animal shelter and I could leave it here.'

Dad bent over, opened the basket and picked the cat up. He took a quick look at it. 'It's a she,' he said.

'Ooh. Can I hold her?' asked Caitlin.

Dad nodded and Caitlin gently took the cat from him. It nuzzled into her jacket straight away and started purring. As Caitlin stroked its head, she looked like she was going to purr too.

'So can I leave her here?' asked the lady.

'Oh no, we're not an animal centre …' I began as Caitlin put the cat back in the basket, which she didn't seem to like. When Caitlin closed the basket door, she complained loudly and poked her paw through again.

Dad bent over to look at the cat again and she meowed at him as well.

'She's really trying to tell us something,' said Caitlin.

'Probably that she doesn't like being in the basket,' said Dad. 'Few cats do.'

'Can I leave her with you?' asked Lily. 'I have to get back, see. My son's coming for his lunch with his kiddies.'

'How do you come to have her?' asked Dad.

'She kept coming to my door. She was clearly starving so I fed her a few times. Wolfed the food down. She had no collar on so I've no idea where she's from. I heard that there was a shelter here. Could you find her a home? Seems a sweet creature.'

'Oh no, we're not a shelter. I'm a vet. I see sick animals,' said Dad.

Lily's eyes watered and she looked like she was going to cry. 'But I can't keep her.'

'Have you put up lost cat notices?' asked Dad. 'She might be a cat new to the area who's got lost, or could belong to a neighbour who's got a dog or a new baby.

Cats often leave home in circumstances like that. They don't like change.'

'I haven't got time to put notices up! I did what I could. I've fed her and left water outside. I am an animal lover, but she wants to come in and my old cats wouldn't have that. It's not fair to them.'

Dad could see that she was getting upset. He put his hand on her arm. 'Of course you're an animal lover. You've done your bit. I wasn't doubting that.'

'So can you take care of her? I don't like to think of her out there in this weather, hungry and cold.'

'Me neither,' said Dad. 'Now don't you worry yourself any more. Let me take your details and then the first thing we can do is to see if anyone local has lost her.'

'I can do that,' said Josh. 'I could put up notices on trees and lampposts in the village and—'

'And I could help,' interrupted Caitlin. She gave me a quick look. I knew her volunteering wasn't so much through love of animals as wanting to get to know Josh better. Hmmmph.

Josh didn't notice. 'That would be great, thanks. Come on, we'll get started straight away.' And off they went towards the house leaving me outside. *Hey*, I wanted to call after them. *Caitlin's my new friend, not yours, Josh.*

In the meantime, Dad had taken down Lily's contact details and soon she was on her way back down the lane.

'So what are you going to do with her?' asked Mr O'Neill.

Dad looked down at the basket and the cat looked up and meowed at him, as if asking the same question. Dad chuckled. 'You are one talkative cat.'

'We can't have her in the house,' I said. 'Ginger would go mental.'

'I know,' Dad agreed. 'But we have to put her somewhere.'

The cat was meowing non-stop. I leaned over and picked it up. 'Shh, we'll look after you. No need to cry.' It stopped immediately and wasn't frightened at all. It seemed to sense that I would be kind to it. It started purring and nuzzled my cheek. I glanced up at the window to check that Ginger wasn't looking out, in case he got jealous, and there he was on my bedroom windowsill, giving me a filthy look. I quickly put the black-and-white cat back in its basket and once again she let out a loud cry of objection.

'Why don't you put her in one of the stables?' Mr O'Neill suggested. 'At least she could run around in there a bit and be out of the horrible weather.'

'She'll be lonely!' I said.

Good idea, Mike,' said Dad. "Don't worry, Amy, we'll look in on her. Let's go and make her comfortable, then I'll make us both a cup of coffee.' He looked at me. 'Actually you're not doing anything are you, Amy? Make us a cup of coffee, will you?'

And off they went towards the stables, leaving me standing there alone in the yard. Abandoned by Caitlin, treated like a servant by my dad. I looked up at the house and saw that Ginger was still on the windowsill in my bedroom. He put both paws up to the window as if he wanted to biff them open and, when that didn't work, he sat back looking very cross.

'Exactly how I feel,' I said and stomped in to see what Caitlin and Josh were doing 'Just call me Cinderella,' I said to no one in particular, as I put the kettle on. 'Everybody's servant.'

Chapter Three

Horse Poo City

Dear Diary,

Weather: it be wet and windy, oo ar.

School: good. I like it. Teachers generally OK and everyone else friendly apart from the snooty girls in Year Eight who walk around like they own the place. Getting to know peeps but Caitlin is new BF (not instead of Natalia, but as well as.) The rules are that I am allowed two best friends, from now. I make the rules. I am Queen Rule-Maker in the life of Amy Westall. My mum thinks she is Queen but she is wrong wrong wrong, it's me. And anyway, Natalia lives a million miles away now. She'd understand about Caitlin and want me to have a new friend.

At school today in PSHE, we had to learn how to do the recovery position in case we ever come across someone who is unconscious. Caitlin was my partner. She acted being unconscious very well because she fell asleep. I positioned one of her fingers in her nose which I thought was very funny, but our teacher, Mr Dixon, didn't.

Went to Caitlin's Monday after school. Her house is just off the main road at the bottom of our lane, not too far. It is heavenly. Warm. They have central heating that works and the house is new and shiny with fields behind. Caitlin's dad owns a couple of paddocks behind their garden and that's where he has started growing his vegetables. She has two younger brothers, one is nine, Zack, the other is seven, Joe. Both are annoying. Zack because he hogs the computer and Joe because he wanted to be in with me and Caitlin in her room, listening in to our conversations. Caitlin threw him out so then he went and banged on a drum kit in the room next door. Her mum is a nurse, which I said must be useful if there's anything wrong with you. Nope, Caitlin said. Her mum is apparently very unsympathetic when she's ill and says, 'Get a hot drink, get to bed and get over it.' Sounds like my mum. They both need to do a course on how to be nicer to their daughters.

Animal life at Silverbrook Farm:

6 happy chickens (but only because the cats aren't allowed out — make the most of it, O clucky ones, for soon the furry fiends will be released,) though Dad has made a coop for them and to keep any foxes out.

2 miserable cats: Ginger still isn't allowed out and is getting crosser by the minute. He entertains himself by trying a different sleeping place every day. This morning it was halfway down the stairs and I almost fell over him on my way to breakfast. Dad said that he changes places so often because of a primal instinct to keep moving so that predators won't know where he is. I think he does it because he is trying to find a warm spot in this draughty old house and also because, like everyone else in this family, he likes to be ANNOYING.

Caitlin named our cat-visitor Cola. Like Ginger, Cola's not allowed to roam in case she gets lost again, so she's confined to one of the stables, which she is not happy about. As soon as we open the stable door to take her food, she's right there ready to run out so we have to be very careful. As Dad said, she is one talkative cat and meows almost non-stop whenever anyone is in with her. Caitlin has fallen in love with her and comes by whenever she can to give her cat cuddles and meow back at her. They have long conversations in meow language. Caitlin wraps her up in her scarf and cradles her like a baby, which Cola seems to like.

One evening, I suggested putting Cola in with Ginger to see if they got on — then at least they could be miserable imprisoned cats together. Bad idea. Josh and I took Cola and tried introducing them but, as soon as he saw her, Ginger narrowed his eyes and went into ninja cat crouching position with flattened ears. There was a lot of hissing. Cola is a sweetie, her tail went down and she looked terrified. She looked up at me and made a long me-ooooooow sound as if to say 'Get me out of here!', so I picked her up and put her back in the stable whilst Josh stayed and tried to calm Mr Jealous Ginger Puss down.

'Shame,' I said to Josh later that night, 'because they could have fallen in love and had kittens.'

Josh rolled his eyes. 'Have you been watching lovey-dovey films and have romance on the brain now?'

'No!' I replied.

I am so misunderstood. I just want everyone to be happy and thought that the cats might have been lonely.

I hear raised voices. Mum and Dad. So goodbye

dear diary. C U l8r. I must go and hide in the hall
and eavesdrop.

'We've no cushion of cash to fall back on,' I heard Mum say.

'I know, love,' Dad replied in his weary voice.

'What are we going to do? The bills are coming in and work isn't.'

'We'll get by. We always have.'

'On what – thin air?'

Exit Mum into the kitchen. Slamming of door. *Bang.*

Exit Dad out into the front, where he will probably go and stand in a field and point at fences to make himself feel better. It usually does.

Oh, I hate it when they argue. It's often about money. Mum's the practical one and does all the bills and stuff. I know she was worried before we left Bristol. 'We're taking a big risk with this move,' she told Dad, but he talked her round. *This following your heart thing needs to come with a lottery win*, I thought as I crept back into my room and shut the door. I heard Josh's door click shut across the corridor. Clearly he'd been listening in too.

On Saturday morning, Mum gave me a list of chores to do. Sadly, giving me things to do is her version of

Dad's fence pointing dance and makes her feel better. She is Ms Stricty Pants in our house, Dad is Mr Softie.

First on the list was cleaning out the stables.

'Eeew. Do I have to? They still smell of horse poo from when Mr Watson was alive and kept a horse. Why can't Josh clean them out?'

'Because he has other things to do,' said Mum. 'He's helping your dad in the fields.'

So not fair. I get the smelly jobs in Horse Poo City and Josh gets to roam about in the fresh air like Lord of the Manor.

The look on Mum's face told me that today was not a day for trying to get round her. She had her 'I've got a broom stuck up my bottom and am not feeling jolly at all' face on.

I sighed and went to the utility room at the back of the kitchen, got the cleaning things, then crossed the yard dragging my feet so that anyone watching would know that in fact, I am a prisoner at Silverbrook Farm, have heavy iron manacles chained to my ankles and it is an ENORMOUS effort to pull my legs along.

Sadly no one was watching. I sighed again and went into the stable next to the one where Cola was. There were about a million years' worth of cobwebs in there. Yuck. I really didn't want one of them on my face so I went back out and crossed the yard, dragging my feet behind me again. I found my bobble hat and a scarf in the hall, wound the scarf around my face and went back to the stable, once again dragging my feet. I felt I was getting rather good at it and made a mental note to demonstrate the chained prisoner walk to Caitlin. I knew she'd appreciate it.

The kitchen window opened. 'Haven't you started yet?' called Mum. 'And why are you walking in that strange way?'

'I'm pretending I have chains around my ankles and am a prisoner,' I called back.

'Welcome to the club. Now stop messing about and get on with it,' she replied.

My talents are wasted on this family. I set about brushing the cobwebs away and, while I was doing it, I decided to change my fantasy from prisoner in chains to being a tiny creature stuck inside my own brain. I often make up stories to help me get through difficult or boring times. Some people think I'm mad, but it helps. I decided to imagine that the stable was my brain and the cobwebs were all the parts that made me feel frustrated and clogged up. I set to the task with super speed and, an hour later, the stable was looking brilliantly tidy (if I do say so myself). My brain felt pretty great too. I stood back to admire my work and noticed for the first time that apart from the Eau de

Horse Poo scent, it was a good space. I went back into the yard. There were six stables. My newly cleaned out brain pinged with a brilliant idea. If Mum and Dad were so worried about money, why didn't they rent out the stables? There must be loads of people with horses and nowhere to put them. I got an image of horses sitting on chairs at the dinner table with knives and forks in their hooves, or propped up in the bath at bath-time having their backs scrubbed, or sleeping top-to-tail with someone and the person being pushed out of the bed because the horse was taking up all the space. I started to laugh.

Mum came out of the kitchen. 'What's so funny?' she asked.

'Oh er … horses,' I replied. 'I was just thinking, what if you had one and nowhere to put it?'

Mum looked blank. 'And that's funny?'

'It is in my head. Listen, I've just had a BRILLIANT idea. Why don't you rent out the stables? Mr Watson used to have a horse here and now the stables are empty. Apart from Cola, that is, and a ton of spiders.'

Mum didn't say anything for a few moments. 'Maybe. Yes, maybe you have something there. But we're not really horsey people, Amy.'

'We could be,' I said. 'I've always wanted to learn how to ride. I could even have my own pony.'

Mum rolled her eyes. 'As if we don't have enough on our plates at the moment with two cats and those chickens. Anyway, what do we know about horses? You probably have to have a special licence or something or … a stable manager. Yes, we'd need a stable manager and that would mean a wage to pay as well as food for horses. So – no, good idea but I don't think it's practical. We can't afford to pay someone.'

'What about a dog then? I've always wanted a dog.'

Mum sighed her weary sigh and gave me a *look* – the one that says 'Don't push your luck, matey'.

So that was that. Water poured on my bright idea. Story of my life. I have mind-bogglingly brilliant ideas and people find a reason to either a) laugh (as in my turn the stables into a leisure park idea) or b) find reasons to dismiss them as unpractical.

One day I will show the world that my ideas are genius ones and then they will all be sorry for not taking me more seriously. Oh yes.

Chapter Four

Trump Town Blues

In the afternoon, I was given time off from all the slavery for good behaviour and headed off to meet Caitlin at the end of our lane. It was a cold bright day and we decided to catch the bus and see where all the other people our age hung out at weekends.

'I was talking to Marie Peters in Year Eight,' said Caitlin, 'and she told me the beach is where *everyone* goes. There's probably a café there and surfers' club and maybe even volleyball we could join in with. Should be good.'

I had my doubts about the beach because it was still February, but Caitlin was so keen to go, and I didn't want to be lame. Plus it might be cool to meet some new friends.

'So the plan is Mission Meet the Locals,' said Caitlin, 'find out where the hotspots are.'

I saluted. 'All aboard, Captain. You lead, I will follow'

Caitlin saluted back. Luckily we didn't have long to wait for a bus and the journey to the coast only took about twenty minutes.

The sky was starting to cloud over, but I kept my mouth zipped. There might be a café. We could get hot chocolates and check out the scene for better days.

We gazed out the window, chatting and taking in the passing scenery, and saw that there were some stunning-looking houses only a short distance from the village. They looked like they were owned by multi-squillionnaires, with terraced lawns and huge patios. Some had swimming pools and one even had a tennis court.

'My future home,' said Caitlin, as we passed a Tudor-style detached house within acres of garden. A teenage girl and an older man, both on horses, waited in a side lane until the bus went past. 'Look, Amy – that girl goes to our school. She must live in one of those mega houses.'

The girl glanced at the bus then looked away.

'She's one of the snooty girls,' I said. 'She's in—'

'I wish I lived in a fantabulous house like that with loads of dosh,' Caitlin interrupted. 'Mum keeps telling me that we don't have any until Dad gets his business up and running. Might take ages though. First he has to wait for his veg to grow and then he has to "find an outlet for his produce".'

"My mum just wants to get a job, any job,' I said. 'She's tried a few places but no joy. Her and Dad argue a lot about money. I had a brilliant scheme to rent out the stables, but as with all my ideas, she totally shut it down.'

'She might be right. A lot of people with horses have their own stables. But maybe you could use them for something else. And if things don't work out, we could all go and live in there, free from the boring grown-ups. We could be like the baby Jesus and Mary and Joseph.'

'Except ours would be a Nativity scene with two grumpy cats and loads of chickens.'

'That's OK. We could dress up in the parts and charge people to come and look. I could be Mary and Josh could be Joseph, Ginger could be Jesus and Cola could be a camel.'

'Exactly,' I said. 'All you need is some imagination.' I was pleased to realise that Caitlin had as much of that as I did. It was a shame our parents didn't.

When we got off the bus, there was a group of boys hanging about at the bus stop, smoking and making odd noises. I didn't like the look of them and was about to set off when I saw that Caitlin was hovering. I should have known. There were three of them, a tall one with hair combed over his face, a ginger-haired boy, and a small blond one with a sweet spaniel by his side. The boys looked a bit gormless to me, not my type at all, though I'm not sure yet exactly what my type is because I don't really like boys that much. As far as I'm concerned, they're just annoying or stupid and sometimes both.

I went to stroke the spaniel, who wagged its tail happily at the attention and made me wish all over again that Mum would let me have my own dog. I listened in for a moment and heard the boys burp. I soon realised that the noises we'd heard when we got off the bus had been burps and they were having a contest to see who could do the loudest one. The tall nerdy-looking boy then did a loud fart and soon after the ginger-haired boy did the same.

The blond boy grinned at me. 'Welcome to Trump Town,' he said.

'Eeeewww,' I said and pulled on Caitlin's arm. 'Come on, Caitlin.'

Caitlin asked for directions to the beach and the tall one pointed us in the direction of a lane to our left while looking at us as if we were mad.

'We're not going swimming,' Caitlin said. 'We're not *that* daft.'

'Don't you want to stay and join in the competition?' asked the blond boy.

'Er … think I'll pass,' I said.

The ginger-haired boy laughed. 'Pass. Pass wind!'

All of them cracked up at this as though I'd said the funniest thing ever.

'*So* juvenile,' I said as we set off down the lane, 'boys are so stupid. Did they really think we'd be impressed by their farting ability? *Je despair.*'

'*Moi aussi,*' said Caitlin. 'But I'm sure there are some decent ones around here somewhere.'

'Maybe,' I said. 'But not if Team Trumpers from Trump Town are anything to go by.'

Soon we could smell the salt air of the sea and hear the roar of the ocean, but it was hard to walk against the wind. It kept blowing into our jackets making them billow out behind us, which gave us a good laugh until I almost took off into the air.

At the end of the lane, I thought another gust was going to knock me off my feet, but at last we could see the sea. It was wild and stormy with massive grey waves crashing on to the shore. I looked up and down the beach. It was completely deserted and there was no sign of a café or a surfers' club or shelter. It started to rain and before long both mine and Caitlin's hair was plastered to our foreheads and Caitlin's mascara dripping down her cheeks. So much for meeting new people and making friends.

Caitlin looked at me and laughed. 'We're the Soggy Girls from Sog City.'

'I suggest we abandon the mission, Captain,' I shouted.

Caitlin pulled her jacket tight around her. 'Suggestion accepted,' she called back. 'Let's get out of here. I am freezing.'

We ran back to the bus stop as fast as we could and luckily Team Trumpers had moved on. We caught the next bus back and, bliss, it was warm inside so we could dry off a bit. 'We need a hot chocolate by a toasty fire,' said Caitlin. 'The seaside isn't much fun during a flipping downpour, is it?'

'Brrr, no,' I replied. 'I thought you said Marie Peters said it was where everyone hung out.'

Caitlin looked sheepish. 'Er … she might have meant in the summer. But there has to be somewhere everyone goes in winter besides hanging out at freezing cold bus stops. Maybe a café?'

We trawled the village for a café but only found shops: a hardware store, pharmacy, newsagent's, post office, mini-supermarket and a pub.

'We could try the park,' said Caitlin, pointing in the direction of some trees. 'It's by the river. There's bound to be a café in there.'

The rain had softened into a drizzle so we put up our hoods and headed off. The park was no more than an expanse of lawn leading down to the river. No sign of a café. There weren't many people about, but we could hear raised voices coming from down near the river.

'Shall we check that out?' said Caitlin. 'Someone might be in trouble.'

We crept nearer and hid behind a tree – a girl and a boy, a few years older than us, were having a row.

'Lovers' tiff?' I whispered to Caitlin.

'I recognise that girl. She goes to our school,' said Caitlin. 'I think she's called Poppy. I heard that her dad is some bigwig at the council.'

'Not very friendly,' I said. 'She's another of the snooty girls.'

'Look, the boy's got something in his hand, a bag and – it seems to be moving on its own.'

'Something is alive in that bag!' I said.

'Either that or it's a good trick,' said Caitlin.

'You were going to drown that!' we heard Poppy say, her voice raised even more.

It was then I saw a tiny tabby face peek out of the bag. 'Oh my God, Caitlin, it's a kitten,' I said.

'I was trying to save it, you idiot,' said the boy, just as angrily as Poppy. 'I saw a man getting ready to throw it in the river! He ran off when he saw me coming – then I heard meowing.'

Just at that moment, Caitlin stepped on a twig and the couple turned to look at us.

'Is someone there?' asked the boy.

'What shall we do?' I whispered.

Caitlin shrugged. 'Not sure, but we have to make sure that kitten is OK.'

I took a deep breath and stepped out from our hiding place. 'I … er … we heard voices.'

Poppy and the boy stared at us.

'Snooping?' asked the boy. He looked about fourteen and, although he had a nice face, he had a surly expression.

Caitlin stepped out to join me. 'We thought someone might be in trouble.'

'Someone was,' said the boy. 'This kitten. A man was going to chuck it in the river and now this silly girl is trying to blame me.'

'Don't you call me a silly girl,' retorted Poppy. She was dressed in skinny jeans and the kind of tweed jacket that horse riders wear.

I walked towards them. 'Well, it's safe now.'

'Yeah, exactly,' said the boy. 'Who are you, anyway?'

'Amy Westall,' I said.

'And I'm Caitlin O'Neill.' Caitlin extended her hand with an over-dramatic flourish. 'Who are *you*?'

'None of your business,' said the boy. 'Do you always eavesdrop on people's conversations?'

'It was hardly a conversation—' I started to say.

'*Everyone* knows who you are,' said Poppy to the boy. 'You're Liam Fisher. Everyone in the village knows your family. Well, your dad, anyway.'

Liam's face went red, but he didn't respond.

'What are you going to do with that kitten?' asked Caitlin.

Liam looked down at the bag and the little worried face peeking out. 'Not sure yet. I'll think of something.' He jumped on to a skateboard by his feet and sped off, taking the tabby kitten with him.

'Bring that kitten back right now!' Poppy called after him. 'I don't trust you with it!'

'Your problem, not mine, Princess Perfect,' he called back over his shoulder.

'I know I've only just met him, but I don't think he'd hurt an animal,' I said, 'especially a kitten. He seemed very annoyed that you thought he was a kitten-drowner. He's probably taking it somewhere safe.'

As I said this, I heard the scrape of skateboard

wheels getting louder again. Liam had turned around and now shoved the bag at me. 'No, I wouldn't hurt it.' He looked pointedly at Poppy. 'But here, you take it, Westall. Your dad's the new vet, isn't he? You're one of the animal rescue people. You sort it out.' He turned to Poppy. 'Satisfied now?'

'I can't take it, Liam,' I said. 'We're not a rescue centre!'

'Your problem, not mine,' said Liam. He appeared to like that line. He sped off again.

'Eugh – that boy is so annoying!' said Poppy. 'He's always in trouble of some sort around the village. I honestly think he *was* going to drown that poor cat.'

'I believe him,' Caitlin said. 'I saw the way he looked at the kitten, his expression was kind. OK, so he could learn to be nicer to people, but I think he was trying to save it.'

'Me too,' I agreed.

Poppy tossed her head back and looked down her nose. 'You're new here, aren't you? What do you know?'

'Who cares about what we know or don't?' said Caitlin. 'It's the kitten that matters. Poor thing. It needs feeding and warming up somewhere quiet.' She took the kitten from me and began stroking it. Her face had gone all soppy and I could see that she'd fallen in love with the little fluffball.

Further along the pathway, Liam had stopped and was watching us. He turned and came back towards us on his skateboard. In a flash he took the kitten from Caitlin. 'If you airheads are going to stand here all day gossiping about me, I'll take it. Your mate here is right. It needs looking after and feeding.'

And off he went again.

'Bring it up to our house later, Liam,' I called after him. 'My dad will sort something out. I promise.' I knew Mum wouldn't be pleased, seeing as we already had Cola, but I was sure that Dad wouldn't turn the kitten away.

Poppy let out a deep sigh of exasperation. 'Fat lot of help you two were,' she said and began to walk off in the opposite direction, but not before giving us a filthy look.

'Nice to meet you too!' Caitlin called after her.

'Let's go and get a hot chocolate,' I said when Poppy and Liam had gone. 'I hate arguments.'

'Me too,' said Caitlin, though I suspect that the drama queen in her doesn't mind a bit of a showdown. She linked her arm through mine and we set off back to the village.

'Over there,' said Caitlin, squinting at a shop window. 'Looks like there's a place you can get a drink at the back of the supermarket. Though it's hardly Café Coolsville.'

I followed as she marched into the slightly shabby supermarket and made her way to the café at the back. We looked at the customers seated at a couple of tables. Most of them were old people.

'Hmm,' said Caitlin, then she turned to the blonde girl at the till whose badge said *Rosie*. She looked a few years older than us and very bored.

'Where are all the people our age?' I asked.

Rosie, who was chewing gum, shrugged. 'Probably at home if they've any sense. It's freezing out.'

'But isn't there anywhere cooler to go?'

Rosie snorted. 'Round here? You have to be joking. I guess some kids go into Weston-super-Mare on a Saturday, but it's miles away. Only one bus a day and no late one back.'

'Where did you go when you were our age?' asked Caitlin.

'Dunno. Nowhere. Friends' houses.'

'What about the beach?'

'Yeah. It's good in summer. Not in this weather though. Only a mad person would go to the beach in this weather.'

I glanced at Caitlin. She grinned. 'Mug of hot chocolate, Mad Person Number One?'

'Don't mind if I do, Mad Person Number Two.'

'You new round here?' asked Rosie.

Caitlin nodded.

'Where do you live?'

'Palcot Street,' said Caitlin.

'And I live at Silverbrook Farm,' I said.

'Oh yeah. I heard there were new people up there. It's an animal rescue home, isn't it?'

'No. It's not a rescue home. My dad's a vet.'

'Not what I heard,' said Rosie. 'I heard it was an animal rescue centre.'

Second person today, I thought. 'No, I think people must have got confused.'

Rosie shrugged again and took our order. We got our hot chocolates and went to sit amongst the other customers, who were all staring at us like we were aliens. Caitlin grinned and waved at a couple, who turned away.

I felt disappointed with the day so far. Even though I was with Caitlin, I'd hoped to find somewhere fun to hang out. Not the kind of fun that involved farting competitions, drowned kittens, and grumpy people like Liam and Poppy.

I sighed. 'In Bristol, there were awesome places to hang out. Cinemas, cafés, loads of cool shops.'

'Same in Swindon,' said Caitlin. She shrugged.

51

'Maybe this *is* it. Maybe as that boy said, welcome to Trump Town.'

'If you can't beat them, join them,' I said and did a fake burp.

Caitlin did the same, only hers was louder.

Chapter Five

Love at First Sight

Mr O'Neill gave Caitlin and me a lift back from the village. As we pulled up the drive, I could see one of the stables doors open, and Mum, Dad and Josh bent over something inside. 'What's going on?' I asked, as the three of us traipsed over. Caitlin had spotted Josh, so there was no stopping her. Gross. Mum had her glum face on. Uh-oh. I hoped she hadn't been arguing with Dad again.

I soon saw what they were looking at. It was the most adorable white-gold puppy in a basket. 'Ohmigod! He's *beautiful*,' I said as I knelt down to put my hand in to stroke his soft fur.

'He's a she, a golden retriever,' said Dad.

'Can I hold her?' I asked, bouncing on my knees with excitement. Dad glanced at Mum and she rolled her eyes, then nodded. I opened the basket and the puppy crawled out, looked at all the faces staring down at her, then leaped on to my knees. She was so cute I could hardly breathe. She put her paws up on my shoulders and started licking my face with great enthusiasm. I gave her a cuddle and she wriggled happily in my arms.

'I think she likes you!' said Dad.

'Who is she? Where's she come from?' I asked, snuggling into her fur again.

'A woman brought her here this morning. She'd only had her a few weeks then heard that her mum is ill so has had to go away to take care of her.'

'To New Zealand,' added Josh. 'She might not be back.'

'Apparently word has got round the village that we're running an animal rescue centre.' *Ah, so that explains the glum face*, I thought. *I'd better not say anything about Rosie in the café saying the same thing.*

Too late.

'It's true,' said Caitlin. 'We were in the café in the supermarket and the girl behind the counter said the same – that Silverbrook Farm is an animal rescue centre.'

Oops.

Mum let out an exasperated sigh. 'You have to stop

this rumour, Richie,' she said, 'before it gets out of hand.'

I looked down at the puppy, who had settled herself on my knees, her tail wagging like mad. 'But what will happen to her?'

'Not just her,' said Dad. 'Since you left this morning, a little boy brought a bird with a damaged wing, and some kid on a skateboard brought a kitten that he found by the river. Unthinkable that someone would try to dump a poor defenceless kitten, isn't it?'

Mr O'Neill nodded. 'But lots do.'

'We saw him,' I said. 'He was arguing with a girl from our school.'

'Did you tell him to bring it here?' asked Mum.

I glanced at Caitlin. Both of us had gone red. 'Not exactly. I ... er ... I did tell him we weren't a rescue centre, but he seemed to have heard the rumour too.'

Mum let out a deep sigh. 'So you *did* tell him to bring it here?'

'Er ...' I tailed off.

'Where's the kitten?' asked Caitlin, saving me.

'In one of the stables,' said Josh. 'Dad's already looked at the bird. It's in the clinic and it's going to be fine. Great, isn't it?'

'No,' said Mum. 'It's *not* great. Am I the only person around here with any sense? Animals and birds need feeding, need warmth. We can't keep them. It's a clinic, not a sanctuary.'

'Actually, could I take a look at the cat that was brought the other day?' asked Mr O'Neill, then gave Caitlin a wink. 'Caitlin won't shut up about it at home.'

Caitlin's face lit up. 'It's a she, Dad. Cola!'

'Sure,' said Dad. 'Come this way. I put the kitten in with her and they seem to get on. It's brought out Cola's maternal instincts.'

Caitlin and Mr O'Neill went off with Dad, leaving me with Mum and Josh and the golden puppy, who every now and again nuzzled my hand and gave it a lick. 'What's her name?'

'Shimmer,' said Josh. 'The lady who brought her said she was like a shimmer of gold in her life. She was really sad to leave her. She was crying, wasn't she, Mum?'

Mum nodded and looked around as if she didn't know what to do. 'Yes, yes, she was, but it was wrong of your dad to agree to take her. What are we going to do with her?'

The puppy let out a soft whine and looked up pleadingly at us. 'Oh, can we keep her, please, Mum?' I begged. The minute I'd seen Shimmer, it had been love at first sight. 'I promise I'll look after her and take her for walks! There's loads of space round here, it will be perfect for a dog. Pleeeease!'

'No,' said Mum firmly. 'Absolutely not. It's not just a question of walking her, it's feeding her too. We can't take on any other commitments until we have some regular money coming in.'

Shimmer's head sank down as if she understood. She looked up at me with sad eyes. 'Oh Mum, how can you resist that face?' I said. 'And she's only a puppy, a *baby*. She probably won't eat much.'

Mum looked torn. 'She's already scoffed down a whole tin of food!' she said, walking off towards the kitchen. 'This is *not good*,' she called back over her shoulder. 'First Cola and now a new lot this morning, heavens knows what the next few weeks are going to bring!'

Caitlin came skipping out of the stable followed by her dad.

'Dad says we can have Cola,' she said, '*and* the kitten. I'm going to call her Pepsi. It would be a shame to separate them. Come and look, Amy! And you, Josh.'

I put Shimmer back in the basket, though she wasn't keen to go, whimpering her objection. 'I'll be back soon,' I promised her. Josh and I followed Caitlin into the stable where the tiny tabby kitten was curled up next to Cola. They were funny to watch. Cola had one paw firmly on the kitten's neck, to make sure she didn't get away, and was giving her ears a thorough cleaning. 'See, they've bonded,' Caitlin said. 'Meow, Cola.'

Cola looked up at Caitlin. '*Meow*,' she seemed to reply.

Caitlin grinned. 'See. She understands me.'

I knelt down to stroke the black-and-white cat and little tabby kitten. They were both purring loudly. 'I looked up at Dad. 'See, it's not so hard running an animal sanctuary. We've found a home for the cats already!'

Dad grimaced. 'Yes it is a bit of luck. Beginners' luck though, Amy. It's not always so easy homing animals. I'll go and find a box to put them in. I've got some with air holes in them in the clinic. Josh, see if you can find an old T-shirt to put at the bottom of the box, so they're comfortable on the ride to their new home.'

After Caitlin and her dad had gone, I went back to Shimmer and gave her a few more strokes. She scrabbled at the basket, but I wanted to go and talk to Mum about her before I let her out again. When I went to the stable door, she whimpered as if to say, 'Don't leave me in here.'

'I *have to*, Shimmer,' I said. 'But only for a while. I

have to go and work on Mum.' But she looked so sad and helpless with her little furry paw up on the basket door, that I couldn't resist.

'Well … maybe we could have you in the boot room next to the kitchen and close the door so that Ginger doesn't see you.'

I picked up the basket and carried it across the yard and into the small room where we kept our wellies and shoes.

'Mum!' I called. 'I'm just putting Shimmer in the boot—'

Mum appeared at the door and pointed the way back to the yard. 'Out, Amy. Take Shimmer back to the stable. You can't afford to get attached to her. Put her back then come back in here. I want to talk to everyone.'

It was hopeless to try and persuade Mum in the mood she was in, so I reluctantly returned Shimmer to the stable. It felt so mean to leave her in there, but I wasn't going to give up. As for not getting attached to her, it was *way* too late for that. Shimmer was *so* cute.

As soon as I'd set foot back inside the house, Mum called me into the kitchen. 'Amy. In here. Family conference. Now.'

I went through to see Josh and Dad already seated

at the table. We exchanged knowing glances as I went to join them. We all knew what a family conference meant – we were in for a lecture.

'So,' Mum began, 'this has to stop – and it has to stop now. Word will be out around the whole county soon, never mind the village. People *cannot* bring their animals here unless they are ill or injured, and then they must take them away with them again. We're running a business, not a shelter.'

'But Mum,' said Josh, 'we've already found a home for Cola and the new kitten.'

Mum looked surprised. 'You have?'

'Yes, Caitlin and her dad took them. They're gone,' I said. 'So that just leaves Shimmer and the bird, so maybe we can—'

'No, Amy, I told you once.'

'But—' Dad started.

Mum gave him a stern look. 'Richie, I know how you feel about animals, and I don't want to be the mean one here, but we have to be *practical*.' Mum was always saying that. Practical generally meant saying no to something fun in my experience.

Mum sighed. 'It's not fair that I always have to be the one that makes the rules.'

'Yes, but we had always thought we'd get a dog when we were settled and—' Dad said.

'*No*, Richie. We're not settled and the practice isn't bringing in enough money to feed strays.'

I glanced over at Josh. He looked as uncomfortable as I felt.

'I know you're right, love,' said Dad, 'but I've been thinking. I wish we *could* make it work. There are no rescue centres for miles. Where are the unwanted animals meant to go? Like that puppy? We have the space and we couldn't see her out on the street. Plus she does seem to have taken a liking to Amy.'

'*No*, Richie.'

I got up. I'd had enough. 'I think you're being horrid, Mum. All you ever say is no. Shimmer is frightened and sad. She must wonder what on earth has happened. She needs love and someone to belong to. I'm going to go and see her.'

'No you're not. It's suppertime soon,' said Mum, 'and I want you to lay the table. Don't worry, I'll make sure Shimmer is fed tonight but *we are not keeping her.*'

'I don't want any supper. You can give mine to Shimmer!' I said and with that, I got up to go.

'Amy, sit down now! You're not going back over to that stable. Richie, tell her. If she gets attached to Shimmer, there will be tears.'

Dad looked torn. 'Amy, do as your mother says,' he said. 'Sit down.'

Mum got up from the table. She looked upset. So did Dad and Josh.

I sat back down. 'I hate it here. It's muddy and rainy and boring and miserable. I wish we'd never moved!'

Chapter Six

Sneaking Out

'Who wants crisps, elderflower cordial and a DVD, maybe a good comedy?' asked Mum later that evening. I knew she was trying to cheer us all up, but I was not in the mood for a jolly family evening – my heart was over in the stable with Shimmer.

I went up to my room and checked my emails. Caitlin had sent me one with a photo of her sitting in their living room with Cola and Pepsi on her lap. She looked so happy, and I couldn't help feeling a little bit jealous. She'd been allowed pets and I hadn't. *So unfair.* I emailed Natalia. I poured everything about the day out to her – the deserted beach, the Trump Town boys, the miserable café, nowhere to go to hang out, the endless rain, the mud everywhere, feeling lonely despite meeting Caitlin, Mum and Dad arguing, Mum not wanting lost or stray animals brought here, and lastly about Shimmer. An email came back a minute later:

To: Chumbuttie@hotmail.com
From: DiamondDiva@gmail.com

My darlink chumbuttie,
   I am so sorry. I wish I was there with you and I wish you could keep Shimmer. Send me a photo of her. My gran always says never give up. Isn't there some way you could make it work? I will have a think. Hey, I don't need to. Pingalata. My brain's just pinged me a brilliant idea. I know what you can do. Ohmigod. I'm going to call you. No I'm not. Mum's calling me. Got to go. Call you soon. I think I know what you can do. Call you later. I am a genius. Natalia XXXXXXXX

Maybe she's going to suggest I run away, I thought. *Not a bad idea*. Although if anyone could come up with a solution to our problems, it was Natalia. She was fantastic at coming up with plans. She wanted to be a businesswoman when she grew up and was forever watching programs on TV about how to run your own empire. I used to tease her about it but she always said, 'You won't be teasing me when I'm a multimillionaire, you loser.' She probably would be too. Just before I left Bristol, she started a baby-sitting agency with her elder sister. They took a small commission and were soon raking in the money – and I don't think she or her sister had to actually babysit once themselves. She was always on the committee organising the school fêtes or Christmas jumble sales.

I switched on my mobile ready for her call, then got into my pyjamas and dressing gown. I wanted to look out at the stable and opened the window a little. A blast of cold air hit me. *Brrr.* It was like opening a fridge door. I hated to think of Shimmer on her own in the dark, freezing stable. She'd be bewildered and wondering where her owner was and what had happened. Poor thing. Then I heard her crying. It got louder and sounded so sad I couldn't bear to listen.

I closed the window and went out into the corridor. I could hear Mum and Dad getting ready for bed, so I went back into my room and waited a bit longer. When the house was quiet, I put on an extra pair of socks, my shoes and a fleece under my dressing gown then scooped up my duvet from the bed.

I found a torch from my bedside cabinet then crept down the stairs, *creak, creak, creak.* Had anyone heard me? Nothing. I carried on down and into the kitchen, got some ham out of the fridge, grabbed a torch from the kitchen drawer then let myself into the boot room and out into the yard. It was so dark, even though the navy-black sky above was full of stars. I switched on the torch and tiptoed across the yard to the stable. I could still hear Shimmer crying, poor baby. I glanced up at Mum and Dad's window and saw that the lights were off. They were probably fast asleep. *Hearts of stone*, I thought. *How can anyone sleep when a creature nearby is frightened and lonely?*

I let myself into the stable and shone the torch. Shimmer was curled up in the corner. At least someone had been in to let her out of the basket, probably Dad. As soon as she saw me, she ran towards me. I knelt down and she jumped on to my knees, paws up on my shoulders, and rested her head on my chest. She soon sniffed out that I had something in my hand for her to eat so I gave her the ham. She ate it so fast, she got the hiccups.

'You have to learn to eat slower,' I said to her, chuckling. She wagged her tail in reply. 'You could knock someone over with that tail of yours, Shim!' After a while she settled on my knee, but kept looking up at me with big, scared eyes.

'You don't have to worry now, Shimmy Shim,' I said.

'I don't care what happens, but you're not going to be on your own any longer.'

I pushed her off for a moment and laid my duvet down on some hay in the corner, then wrapped myself up. I was glad I'd cleaned the place out earlier and tried not to think of scary spiders. Shimmer soon got the idea and came and snuggled under the duvet with me. Again, she laid her head on my shoulder. I looked down at her and felt a burst of love. 'I know exactly how it feels to land in a strange place and be alone and scared, Shimmer,' I said. In coming to Silverbrook Farm, I had been taken away from all that was familiar and I'd felt lonely and isolated. I felt tears come to my eyes. Shimmer put a paw up to my cheek and I cuddled her closer. 'You and me, Shim. We can make it through together and *nobody* is going to say otherwise.'

It was cold in the stable but the heat from Shimmer's soft body kept me warm and I started to doze off. Shimmer relaxed too – no longer crying now that someone was with her.

I woke to hear the sound of the door opening. Someone was coming into the stable! A torch flashed into my eyes. 'Amy!'

It was Mum. Uh-oh.

'What are you doing here?' she asked.

'What are *you* doing here?' I replied.

She looked sheepish. 'I … er … couldn't sleep. I wanted to check that Shimmer was OK.'

Hmm, maybe she hasn't got a heart of stone after all, I thought, but I kept my arms around the puppy, who had also woken up and was looking around to see what was going on. 'She's OK now,' I said. 'But she was crying. I could hear her from my bedroom.' I looked at Mum accusingly.

Footsteps told us someone else was up and a moment later, Dad appeared at the stable door. He took in the situation in front of him. 'Right,' he said. 'Everyone back in the house. It's freezing out here and you'll catch your deaths of cold.'

'I'm not leaving Shimmer,' I said. 'She was frightened and lonely.'

Dad glanced at Mum. 'Shimmer can come too – but just this once,' he said. 'I'll go in first and make sure Ginger is in with Josh, then you can take her up to your room. Make sure you keep the door shut.'

I looked over at Mum. For once, she didn't object.

Chapter Seven

A Plan Is Hatched

'Breakfast!' Mum called.

The smell of bacon and sausages wafted up the stairs. Yum. Shimmer got down from the bottom of my bed where she'd spent the night. She wagged her tail happily, went to the door and scrabbled to get out.

I laughed. 'So you know what the word "breakfast" means, hey? Or is it the smell you like? But I'll have to bring yours up here, Shimmer. We have to keep you away from our mad cat, Ginger, who thinks he owns the place.'

I went down and walked in on Mum and Dad, who were in the middle of an argument. They went quiet when they saw me, but the atmosphere was frosty. Ginger was up on top of the fridge and gave me a disdainful look when I went to sit at the table. He continued staring at me while I ate the plate of scrambled eggs that Mum put in front of me. She sat down and looked at Dad in much the same manner as the cat had looked at me. I hated to think that they'd been arguing and I just had to break the silence: 'I, er, think Ginger knows we have someone else in the house.'

Dad glanced up at the cat, who was still looking down his nose at us. 'He can probably hear and smell Shimmer,' he said. 'And look how he's positioned himself in the highest place in the room as if to show superiority.'

I got up and did a curtsey to Ginger. 'All hail, King of the House, the magnificent and wondrous Ginger.'

Ginger continued to regard me through half-closed eyes. He was not amused. He blinked and looked away as if I was the most boring person on the planet. I shrugged and sat back down at the table. 'Shimmer spent the night curled up at the end of my bed. She is *so* gorgeous. Have you decided what's going to happen to her? Can we keep her? Pleeeeeeease?'

Dad cleared his throat. 'We were just talking about that …' He glanced at Mum. 'We're not sure it's the right time to have a dog yet. Having a puppy is a big commitment.'

'But what will happen to her?' I asked. 'We can't just leave her.'

'She can stay until we find her a home,' said Mum. 'And until then you have to promise to walk her every day, and we have to see how she gets on with Ginger. It is his home after all and he was here first. In the meantime, I'll ask around to see if we can find a suitable place for her to go.'

I almost blurted out, 'But this *is* a suitable home,' but I decided not to push it. *So far, so good*, I thought. *At least Shimmer's out of the stable and in the house, and maybe Mum and Dad will change their minds. Shimmer's so adorable, the more they see her, they're bound to fall in love with her, just as I have.*

'Thank you, thank you. I promise I'll look after her and … if you don't find her a home and decide that we can keep her, that would be so great because I wouldn't feel so lonely any more.'

Mum looked surprised. 'Oh Amy, have you felt lonely?'

'I did when we first got here, but not so much any more because I have Caitlin as a friend now, but some days, I still feel like an outsider. That's why I felt for Shimmer being out there in the stable on her own. I really understood how she must have felt finding herself in a strange place. That's why I wanted to be her friend.'

'Why didn't you say how you felt when we arrived here?' asked Dad.

'What difference would that have made? Everyone was so busy unpacking and talking about chickens or curtains. Anyway, it doesn't matter any more. I have Caitlin *and* Shimmer.' Ginger made a squeaky meow. 'Oh and you too, Ginger, but everyone knows you're Josh's cat.'

'Don't get too attached to Shimmer,' Mum warned, 'we haven't said you can keep her permanently. You do understand that, don't you?'

I nodded, although I knew that I was already attached. And I had a plan to keep her. I was sure that Shimmer was meant to stay with us and, if I behaved, didn't argue with Mum and looked after Shimmer *really* well, Mum and Dad were sure to come round. Shimmer was irresistible.

After breakfast, I went to check on Shimmer and take her some food, then went to the bathroom. I must have left my bedroom door ajar because by the time I got back to my room, Ginger had got in. *Oh no,* I thought, *not a great start to showing how well I can look after the new puppy.* Josh ran in after Ginger, but we were both too slow. The two animals were already checking each other out like cowboys getting ready for a shootout. Ginger had crouched low and was watching Shimmer, who was wagging her tail. I think she thought it was a game because she also crouched low and crawled on her belly slowly towards Ginger then went back to her first position, where she rolled on her back. Dad told me once that when an animal does that, it is showing that it is no threat because it's showing its tummy, its most vulnerable part. Shimmer rolled back up then advanced forward again on her front paws, all the time wagging her tail.

'She wants to be friends, doesn't she?' I said to Josh. He nodded.

Suddenly Ginger sprang forward and biffed Shimmer on the nose with his right paw and with that, he turned and walked out of the room. Shimmer didn't seem to mind at all. She came over to me and leaned against my legs, her tail wagging as it always was.

Josh and I laughed. 'Ginger was letting her know who's the boss,' said Josh.

We went downstairs followed by Shimmer, who seemed very at home already. Ginger was at his bowl eating and at the smell of food, Shimmer went to join him. Ginger promptly biffed her on the nose again so she retreated under the table.

I glanced at Mum and Dad to see if they were going to be cross that Shimmer had got out, but Dad grinned. 'Hey, I think they're going to be all right. Shimmer's caught on fast not to bother Ginger when he's eating, and there was no spitting or hissing. They're just establishing a few ground rules.'

He got up and put out some more food in a second bowl for Shimmer, though was careful to put it at a distance from Ginger, who glanced over at the puppy for a moment then carried on eating his Whiskas. When he'd finished, he went towards the stairs.

'Look,' said Dad. 'Ginger's tail is up, that means he's OK with things. If he wasn't, his tail would be down.'

Excellent, I thought. *That's one hurdle over. If things carry on like this, Mum and Dad'll have no reason not to let Shimmer stay.*

After breakfast, Shimmer and I went back up to my bedroom, where she got busy chewing the shoelace on one of my trainers.

'I think we're going to have to buy you some toys,' I said to her, pulling it out of her mouth. 'Shoes aren't for chewing, and you have to be on your best behaviour for the next few weeks so that I can keep you.'

Shimmer gazed up at me and put her paw on my knee. She was so sweet, I just had to kneel down and give her a cuddle. 'I won't let them send you away,' I said as I nuzzled into her furry neck. 'I won't.'

Shimmer replied with a woof.

'Exactly,' I said. 'Woof, woof.'

I took a quick photo of her with my phone and sent it to Caitlin. She texted back immediately: *Adorable*.

It was then that I saw that there was also a text from Natalia. In all the excitement over Shimmer, I'd forgotten about her saying that she'd call me with her brilliant idea. *Check ur emails*, she'd texted. I went to my desk and opened my laptop. I soon saw her message.

To: Chumbuttie@hotmail.com
From: DiamondDiva@gmail.com

Hello darlink. Check out the link below. Take a look at this place and explorez vous their site. I went there yesterday with Mum and Dad and that's what gave me the idea. Totes fabnostic. You have the perfect location for something similar. In the meantime, I will think up fundraising ideas. L8rs.
   Natalia XXXXXXXXXX

At the bottom, she'd added a web address.

I pressed the link, looked at the home page and scrolled down. At first it didn't make any sense to me, though I did what she had instructed and explored the site. As I clicked through the pages, the penny dropped. I got exactly why she'd sent it. I knew that Caitlin would get it too, so I quickly sent her the link.

I picked up my laptop, went out into the corridor and called, 'Family conference. In the kitchen. Now.'

Haha, I thought as I went down the stairs and almost fell over Shimmer, who ran in front of me on the way. *Mum's not the only one who can call everyone together!*

Soon we were all seated around the table. Ginger had positioned himself at one end, in a position of superiority again, from where he regarded Shimmer. Every now and again, Shimmer would approach the table and try and put her paws up. Each time, she was met with a biff on the nose from Ginger. Shimmer didn't mind at all. She kept going back for more and every time Ginger biffed her, her tail wagged even more. Even Mum had to laugh. 'They seem to be getting along well, don't they?' she commented. 'Probably because Ginger knows Shimmer is a pup and not a threat.'

'Or more likely, even Ginger can't resist Shimmer's cuteness,' I said.

'Hmm, maybe, but cats often establish themselves as the boss in a household,' said Dad. 'So, Amy. What's so important?'

I opened my laptop and clicked on the link that Natalia had sent me then turned the computer around so that everyone could see. 'Natalia sent me this *brill* idea. Check it out.'

'What are we meant to be looking at?' asked Josh as he squinted at the home page.

'Just explore and use your brain, you dingbat,' I said. 'Take your time.'

I let them have a few minutes looking at the site then Mum leaned back and actually smiled. She'd got it. I grinned back at her.

'Not a bad idea ...' said Mum. 'Not bad at all. Better than the horse stables idea.'

The website that Natalia had sent me was for a farm shop and café just outside Bath. The shop was bright and clean with baskets full of gorgeous-looking local produce, fruit, vegetables, herbs, a meat counter, shelves laden with chutney, jam, marmalade, a counter with scrummy-looking homemade cakes. Another page showed a café which was located in a barn, but not like our shabby-looking barns – this one had been decorated and looked authentic, but was spotless and bright with smiling teenagers in green aprons behind the counter.

'And there's more,' I said and pressed through to another page which showed an area with goats and chickens. 'We've got it all here,' I said. 'We have the barns, the stables, the land.'

'Amy, love, this sort of venture costs a lot of money.' Mum had her worried face on again.

I wasn't going to be put off. 'No problem. We'll put together a business plan. Get a loan,' I said. All that watching *Entrepreneur Challenge* with Natalia hadn't gone to waste.

Mum laughed. 'Get Amy – businesswoman of the year.'

'There might even be grants for this sort of thing,' said Josh. He'd sat through endless episodes of *Entrepreneur Challenge* when Natalia had stayed for sleepovers.

'What do you think?' I asked. 'We've already got a tea shop of sorts but imagine if we made it nice and decorated it so that people would actually *want* to come here.'

'Well, I *could* make cakes,' said Mum. 'And jams and chutneys. Start our own business …' She had a dreamy look in her eyes, but then looked round and put her 'we've got to be practical' face on again. 'Maybe …'

'Mr O'Neill could bring his vegetables,' said Josh.

'Good idea, Josh,' I said. 'I don't think there's anything like it around here, Mum.'

Mum nodded. 'There's the supermarket in the

village and the café at the back, but it's not really very nice.'

'If we could make it really fun and pretty, people would come here instead,' I said.

'You're right, farm shops *are* all the rage these days,' said Mum. 'People want to know where their food is grown, where it comes from, what it's been sprayed with.'

'Though it hurts me to say this about my sister,' said Josh. 'I think you might be on to something, Amy. What do you think, Dad?'

I felt a rush of excitement. 'But that's not all,' I said. 'The shop and the café could make money. The money could pay for an animal rescue centre.'

'Running a café and shop *would* see us through times when the clinic is quiet,' said Mum. 'I'm not sure about a rescue centre though, Amy.'

Dad still hadn't said much but I *knew* it was a good idea. I wasn't going to give up. 'People are getting fed up with big supermarkets, and smaller places selling organic produce are becoming really popular. We did a lesson about it at school. And … and … Natalia's going to send me some fundraising ideas. And I bet Caitlin would have some good ones, too. We wouldn't have to rely totally on the shop. We could run events, special sales – I don't know, we'll think of something.

I'm sure people will want to help. What do you say, Dad?'

'It's definitely worth considering,' he said, 'but it would be costly. I just can't imagine how we'd make it work. But let's try putting together a business plan.'

'Natalia could help with the plan,' I said. 'She's a whiz at things like that.'

'How old are you again?' asked Dad.

'Eleven going on forty,' said Mum. 'Richie, I have a good feeling about this. I can see it. "Silverbrook Farm Produce". We need to do some market research and see what the competition is round here. There's bound to be some but, Amy, you're right. I haven't seen anything like it in the local area. Josh, maybe you could design us a logo for the labels and advertising. Something showing the farmhouse, maybe in summer, with roses growing up the arch above the front door so it looks countrified.'

Josh got up. 'I'm on it,' he said. He was brilliant at art and was always designing things on his computer.

Mum got up to get some paper and soon she and Dad were bent over a notepad making lists.

It was a good job they were preoccupied because it was then that I saw that, while everyone had been busy looking at my laptop, Shimmer had helped herself to the sausages that had been left on the side counter. A last gulp, they were gone and Shimmer began to hiccup again.

'Er … while you're doing that, I'll take Shimmer out,' I said and made a quick exit before anyone noticed that their breakfast had disappeared.

Chapter Eight

To the Rescue

March

Dear Diary,

It's been a while since I wrote in here because so much has been going on. Now it's spring and the flowers are poking their heads out of the ground. Project Silverbrook is going ahead. Yay. Everyone's been doing their research, making plans. Mucho excitement in the Westall family.

Silverbrook animals: Ginger has become Hunter Warrior Cat. He's allowed out now and is very happy in his new territory. The downside is he keeps bringing us small furry presents from the fields — mice and small birds. He's not a killer like some cats, but does like to hunt. Dad says he brings his catches in to show he can contribute to the grocery shopping. I've tried telling him we really don't want mouse on toast thank you very much, but he hasn't got the message. We keep a fishing net by the back door and Dad does his best to catch whatever's been brought in, take it back out and set it free.

Shimmer is a joy and my new best friend. She follows me everywhere. When I go to school, she howls like a baby and looks at me with big sad eyes, but then is sitting in the window looking out and waiting for me when I get back and gives me the best, lickiest welcome home ever. Have been on my best behaviour round the house, offered to do washing up, help out where I can, in the hope that Mum and Dad will let me keep Shimmer. I couldn't bear to see her go somewhere else because I have completely fallen in love with her.

We did a class on reincarnation in school last week. Interesting theory that we may have lived before in different bodies. I think Dad was probably St Francis of Assisi, the saint who was kind to animals. I reckon Mum was Attila the Hun. She still has days when she seems in a rage about something or other, but has been a lot better since she's had the Silverbrook Farm

project to work on. They've been working on the
business plan and we have a road trip planned for the
Easter holidays to go and talk to someone in a rescue
centre about an hour away from here. I'm not sure
what Josh was in a past life. Probably a frog. Haha.

Mum has great ideas for the tea shop and has been
in there with an architect drawing up plans. Mrs
Watson wasn't too happy about it but Mum assured
her she'd always have a job, though that didn't seem
to appease her much. We've started opening the tea
shop at weekends to try and make some money before
it gets converted, but not many people come. Natalia
sent us a DVD called Field of Dreams to watch. It's
about a man who builds a baseball pitch after hearing
voices, then a bunch of ghosts turn up and play
baseball on the pitch. Not sure what that had to do
with us starting our venture but it was inspiring in an
odd kind of way. We all go round quoting a line from
the film: 'Build it and they will come.' Apart from
Mum, that is. Her favourite line is 'Shut up or I will
throttle you'.

Word did get round the village that we had started
an animal rescue centre and people began bringing up
animals, but Dad has been v. firm and said not yet,
we're not ready. He has been drinking Mum's sensible
juice, and I guess he's right, though we couldn't resist

keeping some of them – like the Jack Russell called
Rupert. His owner died and he was found all on his
own in a house, and was scared, starving and not well
at all. He's a sweet-looking little dog, with a white
coat with brown patches all over it. He was a bit quiet
when we first brought him home but when he'd been
fed and realised he was safe, his real nature came out
and he was soon running about happily wagging his
tail. Luckily Mrs Watson said she'd foster him until
we're up and running. She's a funny old bat but
obviously has a kind heart.

On the first Saturday in the Easter holidays, we set off
on our road trip. Destination: the rescue home for
dogs and cats. Mum looked very smart in a navy
trouser suit and her hair tied back, and I could see that
Dad had made an effort too because, for once, he
wasn't wearing odd socks, and Shimmer was wearing
a new red collar specially purchased for the trip. And
Mum and Dad said Caitlin could come too, which
would make it double fun.

On the journey, we made up a list of questions to
ask when we got to the centre.

'Ask how much it costs them a year to run the
place,' said Mum.

'Megabucks, I bet,' said Caitlin.

'Where would you find that?' Josh asked.

'Exactly,' said Dad. 'Put that as question number one. How do you find the money to run a rescue centre?'

'It says on their website that people are asked to make a donation when they adopt an animal,' I said. 'That gives some money. We'd have to have a similar site so people can read about the animals, how much it would cost, how to donate. You should take a look, Josh.'

'Already have, dingbat. I could do one for us, easy peasy. We could also use all the social media like Twitter and Facebook. I could update a Facebook page with photos and stories about the centre and animals.'

'Whoa. Slow down, J-boy. First we have to get the funding,' said Dad.

When did he turn into Mr Grumpbucket?

We turned down a narrow lane lined with trees, right into a car park and there it was – a glass-fronted chalet-style building with a patio in front of it. 'Coooool,' said Josh.

'Yeah,' said Caitlin, but she was looking at Josh not the building. As always, he was oblivious to her crush on him. As soon as we got out of the car, we could hear dogs barking in the background.

'You stay here,' I said to Shimmer, who thought she

was getting out with the rest of us. She looked most put out when I closed the door on her, but we wouldn't be leaving her for long, and it wasn't a hot day. I looked around at fields surrounding the centre. *Nice location*, I thought as we made our way to the front and into the airy reception area. It had a counter on the right for people to check in, a pet shop to the left and at the back was a closed glass door that led to the kennels. A friendly-looking man came out and introduced himself as Mazhar.

'Thanks so much for agreeing to meet with us,' said Dad.

'You're welcome,' Mazhar said and indicated that we should sit down at a round table to the front of the reception. Josh, Caitlin and I were dying to get through the doors and see the animals, but we stayed and listened as Mum and Dad began their questions.

I was so busy dreaming of all the animals we'd soon be looking after as hundreds of people came from all over the country to visit our famous tea shop, that I zoned out when Mazhar told Mum and Dad how much the centre cost to run – though I think I heard the word 'millions'. An odd strangled sound came from Dad's side of the table.

'And how do you find that money?' asked Mum.

'Mainly through fundraising,' replied Mazhar. 'We

have a whole team of people working on it. We also rely on donations from the public. We're a registered charity so sometimes we're gifted amounts in people's wills and other times a wealthy individual makes a large donation. We are a nation of animal lovers and people do leave their money – especially those who've been and seen the place, but we have to work hard to raise money for times when there aren't donations.'

That's it, I thought. *It's never going to happen.* I expected Mum to get up and tell Dad that we were wasting our time, but she didn't. She was listening.

'We do cover a very wide area,' said Mazhar, 'six hundred and fifty square miles throughout Somerset and Wiltshire.'

Josh let out a whistle. 'How many animals do you have?' he asked.

'We can house over one hundred and twenty dogs, one hundred and twenty cats, one hundred chickens and fifty or so small animals.'

'That's a lot of space you need,' said Caitlin. I knew she was thinking the same as I was – that there was no way could we get that many into our land and stables.

'We rehome about two thousand animals a year.'

'What?' I cried again. It was getting worse by the minute. That was impossible. I felt my heart sink.

'Amy, be quiet,' said Dad. 'Let's hear what Mazhar has to say before we panic.'

Mazhar smiled. 'A lot of people are surprised when they hear the figures. Money is also raised by businesses, schools, cake sales, local events, marathons– our pet shop makes us some money too.'

I'd taken note of the shop earlier. We hadn't thought about selling pet products and I thought it would be a good addition to the farm shop.

'What happens if you're full?' asked Mum.

'We have a waiting list. It's one in, one out. We have a list of people who are willing to foster animals until we have a place for them and can find them a more permanent home,' he smiled. 'It's really what all of them want, a home and to be loved.' I thought of Shimmer and how happy she was to be part of our family and have somewhere she belonged. I prayed for the hundred millionth time that it would be permanent.

'And how many vets do you have on site?' asked Dad.

'We have one vet and one nurse. All the animals get a health check when they come in – checked for fleas, worms, skin disease as well as getting their vaccinations.'

'What about other staff?' asked Mum.

'We have about forty, some working full-time, some part and we have about three hundred people working here as volunteers – all the dog walkers and cat cuddlers.'

'Cat cuddlers?' said Caitlin, looking excited. Cat cuddling was her favourite pastime.

Mazhar nodded. 'They come in just to do that – and they cuddle the small animals too to let them know that they're safe and not alone, but also to socialise them so when we do find them a home, they're used to people.'

'What happens when they first come in?' asked Josh.

'They're put in an assessment block for seven days while we do what we can to try and find their owner, but of course that's not always possible.'

'Why do animals end up in here?' I asked. I wasn't sure I wanted to know. Whatever the answer was, it was probably sad.

'Oh, all sorts of reasons. Sometimes their owner dies, or is elderly and has to go into a home or hospital. Sometimes it's a couple splitting up, sometimes an accident, or they've been neglected; other times, changes in the household like a new baby or a new job that means an owner can't care for their pet, or lack of funds and people can't afford to keep their animals. We see all sorts of cases, sometimes people just can't cope with the responsibility.' He looked over at the reception area. 'This job can be a bit of a roller-coaster. One moment, it's happy – rehoming an animal and knowing it's gone somewhere safe – and the next having to tend to some poor creature that's been abandoned. A cat was brought in this morning who had been left under a bush by the motorway. Poor thing was traumatised.'

I sat and listened as Mum and Dad continued with their questions, but the more Mazhar told us, the more dejected I felt. The centre was totally amazing, but there was no way our family could pull off something similar unless Dad turned into Harry Potter.

After half an hour, Mazhar offered to show us around and led us into the kennel area. As soon as we got in there, all kinds of dogs appeared at the front of their cages to greet us, some pawing at the mesh, some barking to say hello. A beautiful Irish terrier called Seamus did an amazing jump when he saw us as if to say, *'Wahey, look what I can do!'* Some didn't stir and just looked at us wearily. On each kennel, there was a notice saying the dog's name and a little about their history. As we walked up and down the aisles and looked in, we saw all types and ages of dogs: a spotty Dalmatian, a fluffy collie, yappy little bull terriers, an excitable cocker spaniel, Millie the Shih Tzu (so cute, she was only eight months old), a gorgeous white Husky, a long-legged lurcher, some types I didn't know and one quiet German Shepherd called Bailey who looked up at us with the saddest eyes. I wanted to take all of them home and give them a big hug. Caitlin linked arms with me as we walked around. I knew she found it as hard looking at all the homeless animals as I did.

'I wish we could get a coach and come here and take them all home,' she whispered.

'Me too,' I whispered back, 'but I'm having a hard enough time trying to get Mum and Dad to agree to keep Shimmer.'

'Are there ever animals who don't find a home?' Josh asked.

Mazhar nodded. 'There are a few who have been here over a year, but we do our best to keep them comfortable. We have a no-destruct policy – that means we don't put any animals to sleep unless they're poorly – and as well as the dog walkers who take them out daily, we have an agility area where they can exercise and a place where they can dig too. Dogs do love to dig.'

I noticed that there were hip-height fences wherever we went. 'Why the fences? Is that to stop them getting out?'

Mazhar shook his head. 'No. That's to obscure their view of other dogs. It can be overwhelming for them to see so many other dogs, so the fences give them a little privacy and it stops them getting stressed. Although we do our best, no animal wants to be here in kennels with strange people and strange dogs. Like us, they like the familiar. They just want to belong to someone.'

'I know,' I said and looked at Mum in the hope that she got the message that I was thinking about Shimmer.

'We also have what we call stooge dogs,' Mazhar continued. 'They're like nannies and if a dog is too hyper, we put it in with an older stooge dog who can teach it better behaviour and calm it down. If we have a dog that is shy and scared, we put it in with a stooge dog who can make it feel safe and bring it out of itself a bit.'

'Wow, you've thought of everything!' said Josh.

'Can anyone come and get a dog?' asked Caitlin.

Mazhar shook his head. 'Absolutely not. We screen people carefully. We always do a home visit to ensure that it's a good environment that they're going to, as well as a good match with a new owner. The last thing we want is for a dog to go to a home then get brought back because someone didn't really understand the commitment. It would be too distressing for them.' I gave Mum another look when Mazhar said this. He was making a very good case for us to keep Shimmer. I remembered how upset Shimmer was when she first arrived at Silverbrook Farm. I looked at Caitlin. She put her hand on her heart to show me that she knew what I was thinking.

After the dog kennels, Mazhar took us into the cat area and, once again, there was cage after cage. The cats didn't get up to say hello, they just regarded us through lazy eyes. Max, Charlie, Bindy, Daphne, Mozza, Parker, Graham, Stan – furry face after furry face; black, tabby, white, ginger … a total sweetheart tabby with only one eye, called Snowdrop. I'd like to have taken them all home, along with the dogs.

This time, I had to link arms with Caitlin. I knew how much she adored cats and her eyes had filled with tears. 'I can't bear it,' she said. 'I really really hope Silverbrook animal rescue happens because we have to do what we can to help!'

She let go of my arm and lingered behind as Mazhar led our group on. When I turned round, I could see she was talking to the cat with one eye. 'Don't you worry, baby, someone will come and take you home soon,' she said.

'Cats *really* don't like being in the cattery pens –

they like to run around,' said Mazhar, 'so we work hard to home them as soon as we can – and we do have quite a quick turnaround on finding them places, faster than the dogs.'

'They must feel cooped up in there,' I said, remembering how Ginger acted when he was kept inside. He was one miserable cat.

Mazhar nodded. 'We have an area where we can let them out one at a time so they get some exercise at least and we also play classical music to help keep them calm, and sometimes give them catnip which is a herb they seem to like. We even have someone who comes in and does massage sometimes – on the dogs too, they love it.'

Caitlin ran to catch us up. 'Don't you find it heart-breaking working here?' she asked.

Mazhar smiled. 'Of course I do, especially when I see the cases of abuse or an animal that has been neglected, but at least I am doing what I can – and all of these little guys are such fun to hang out with. Animals are so trusting, dogs will love a person unconditionally if they are treated well – and even sometimes if they aren't. I just try to do what I can to keep them safe and find them homes, so it's a very rewarding job, really.'

By the time we'd finished, I felt sad. So many animals in need of homes and someone to love them.

'I'm glad there are places like this,' I said to Mazhar when it was time to say goodbye.

'Me too,' he said. 'And we need more centres. It's hard work but worth it.'

'Can we stay in touch in case we have any more questions?' asked Dad.

'Of course you can. Best of luck with your venture,' he said.

We need more than luck, I thought as we walked back to the car. *We need a miracle – one that involves us finding a bounty of gold at the bottom of the pond.*

Everyone, even Caitlin, was quiet as we drove away. I cuddled Shimmer extra close and buried my nose in her soft fur. 'You're my girl,' I said, 'and I'm going to make sure nothing bad ever happens to you.' She replied in her usual fashion – by giving me a big wet lick.

Chapter Nine

Chateau D'Espair

Dear Diary,

Silverbrook Farm rescue centre/farm shop/café project update one week after the visit: NOT HAPPENING.

Family mood: It is Chateau D'Espair here. Everyone is mucho glum and silent. Even Josh, who's usually Mr Bright and Annoyingly Perky.

Silverbrook animals: oblivious to the atmosphere. Ginger likes to go exploring now that it's April and the winter is over. Sometimes we don't see him for hours because he is out surveying his new territory and no doubt telling any creature he meets that he is king of the land. Shimmer still eats too fast and gets hiccups – she loves food and eats anything she sees, even bread. One day she got the runs and Dad had to take a look at her and put a thermometer up her bum to check her temperature. Boy, did she let out a yelp! It didn't stop her eating everything in her sight afterwards though. Her favourite food is ice cream. Vanilla. She can't get enough of it. She eats it in one go. No licking and savouring it for her. Gomph. And it's gone. Other favourites are sausages, sausage rolls and crisps – any flavour.

School: is fine. Seems a long time ago since I stood outside feeling nervous. It's cool for a school but nice to be on holiday from it over Easter.

Me: Since our visit to the rescue centre, I feel like I am made from wet sand – and not even getting Easter eggs cheered me up. Shimmer seems to have picked up on this and as soon as I sit down, she comes and sits next to me and puts her head on my knees. But that might be because she wants to eat the Easter eggs. She is one greedy dawg. Now the weather is getting better, I take her down to the beach, which she loves because she can dig the sand there and she adores playing in the waves. So far, Mum and Dad haven't found her another home, though I don't think they've been trying too hard. I don't ask about it because I don't want to remind them of their plan to find her somewhere else.

Late afternoon, I emailed Natalia.

From: Chumbuttie@hotmail.com
To: DiamondDiva@gmail.com

Visit to rescue centre has shown us that we were aiming
way beyond our level. Project abandoned. Boo hoo. We
are the house of Les Miserables here.
    Love
    Amyserable

From: DiamondDiva@gmail.com:
To: Chumbuttie@hotmail.com

Dear Darlink Chumbuttie
    No way. Get up. Get over it. One should always aim
high. Remember that quote: *if a man aims for the top of a
tree, he will get to the lower branches, if a man aims for
the stars, he will reach the top of the tree.*

Huh? I thought.
A second later, another email pinged in.

From: DiamondDiva@gmail.com
To: Chumbuttie@hotmail.com

Dear Dozo
It means always aim beyond your means.
N XXX

It was as if Natalia was reading my mind. I had forgotten how spookily psychic she could be, as well as infuriatingly positive. She was always coming out with quotes she found in her 'think big, change the world, change yourself, conquer the universe' books. She didn't understand. She hadn't heard what Mazhar had told us. We had the facts and Silverbrook Farm animal rescue centre was a non-starter. Mum and Dad had no savings. Dad had little work. The situation was hopeless.

To: DiamondDiva@gmail.com
From: Chumbuttie@hotmail.com

Dear Nat. You are Very Annoying. Love Amy.

From: DiamondDiva@gmail.com
To: Chumbuttie@hotmail.com

Herumph. So are you Annoying, you poo bucket. Don't
give up. Miracles happen but first you have to work hard.
Make plans. There will be a way. Love Natalia

Another of her quotes, I thought. Although highly irri-
tating, I didn't want Natalia to think I was a loser, so
I decided to Google some quotes of my own and send
them back to her. *I will out positive you. Haha, oh yes, let's
see who can have winning attitude.*

I Googled 'quotes for success in business'. Pages and
pages of sites came up. I clicked on the first one and
began to read.

1. Courage is being scared to death, but saddling
    up anyway. ~ John Wayne

Hmm. OK, if you're a cowboy I guess, I thought.

2. If you don't make things happen then things
    will happen to you. ~ Robert Collier

Yeah, like mass family depression. It's like the Temple of Doom round here lately.

3. A business has to be involving, it has to be fun, and it has to exercise your creative instincts ~ Richard Branson

Missed a point there, Richard my man, I thought. It also has to have lots of dosh rolling in. Doesn't he know anything?

4. Whatever the mind of man can conceive and believe, it can achieve. Thoughts are things. And powerful things at that, when mixed with definiteness of purpose, and burning desire, can be translated into riches ~ Napoleon Hill

Yeah. Go Napoleon. Now you're talking.

5. Nothing great was ever achieved without enthusiasm ~ Ralph Waldo Emerson

Try telling that to my parents, Mr and Mrs Grumpbucket. As if to show what real enthusiasm was, Shimmer started to chase her tail and started whizzing round in a circle. It was so funny to watch her going faster and faster trying to catch it.

6. It does not matter how slowly you go, so long as you do not stop ~ Confucius

Unless you are Shimmer chasing her tail, in which case, it is a good idea to stop when you get dizzy, I thought as Shimmer collapsed on the floor, her head spinning. She looked up at me, tongue out, tail wagging. She is one happy daft dog. I do love her.

7. Life isn't worth living unless you're willing to take some big chances and go for broke ~ Eliot Wiggington

Ah, now that's one to show the family, I decided.

8. People become really quite remarkable when they start thinking that they can do things. When they believe in themselves, they have the first secret of success ~ Norman Vincent Peale

9. Twenty years from now you will be more

disappointed by the things that you didn't do
than by the ones you did do ~ Mark Twain

10. The important thing is not being afraid to
    take a chance. Remember, the greatest failure
    is to not try. Once you find something you
    love to do, be the best at doing it ~ Debbi
    Fields

By the time I'd finished reading the quotes, I felt the
stirring of excitement. Natalia had been right. We'd
given up too soon and had to change our attitude. I
copied and pasted the quotes and sent them off to
Natalia. *Stick those in your positive pipe and smoke them*,
I thought as the email disappeared from my outbox. I
read the quotes again.

'We accepted defeat,' I said to Shimmer, who
wagged her tail in response. 'We've been thinking like
losers. There must be a way forward. Other people
have made things work.'

I highlighted the ten quotes I liked the most,
printed them out, then went out into the hall and
called, 'Family conference.' Then I did a trumpet blowing sound. 'Doo do do do dah.'

I went downstairs. No one came. I found Mum
in the kitchen. 'Didn't you hear? I called family
conference.'

Mum shrugged. 'If it's about the project, I don't want to hear,' she said as Dad came through the door.

'Hear what?' he asked.

'I called a family conference,' I said. 'I've been thinking, we gave up too soon. Read these.' I handed Dad the sheet of paper. 'Think about it. Yes, we can't achieve anything like the centre we went to see, but we could create something here. Mazhar told us that they cover over six hundred square miles. We don't have to cover an area that big. We take it step by step. Start small with what we can manage. Please let's not give up yet.'

Dad looked over at Mum. Her expression gave nothing away. 'I had actually been thinking something similar,' he said.

'Me too,' said Josh from the doorway. 'Let's not give up. We could put out feelers, advertise our plan and see if we can get any backers. If we can get the community behind us, word gets out. As Mazhar said, we're a nation of animal lovers, we might get some donations.'

'And pigs might fly,' said Mum, Queen Grumpbucket of the Day.

'That would make a great headline,' I said. 'Especially if we could find some flying pigs.' I flapped my arms like wings. 'Oink, oink.'

Dad and Josh cracked up and even Mum had to smile. 'I suppose everyone has been a bit miserable since we gave up,' she said.

'Understatement,' I said. 'We've been tragic. Les Miserables. Famille Westall de Glumpole.'

'But the real tragedy would be animals that need homes and help,' said Dad.

'Exactly,' I agreed. 'We don't try to do it on the scale of the rescue centre we saw, we do it Westall size, what we can manage here at Silverbrook Farm. And the ideas of the shop and café are still good ones.' I looked at Mum. I knew that was the part of the project that appealed to her most. 'We could make it so fab. We have the location. People will want to come here if we get it right.'

'The press,' said Mum. 'That's where we should start. We could feature a few stories about the kind of animals who are brought to rescue centres, appeal to people's hearts, individual stories about individual cases – the sadder the better – and then we could outline our plans. We can't be the only family in the county that are soft when it comes to animals.'

Dad gave her a surprised look. 'Wow. You've changed your tune.'

'Amy's not the only one who watched TV programmes about how to be a success in business,' she said. 'Us Westalls are winners. And really, what choice do we have? There's still not a lot of work for you, Richie. I haven't got a job. I'm tired of feeling grumpy. I want to move on and be positive. I love the idea of running our own business and I reckon I could create a great shop and café.'

I went and gave her a hug. 'Now you're talking.'

Mum made sandwiches, a pot of tea and we spent the rest of the evening brainstorming ideas. Some were mad, some were sensible, but as the evening went on, a list was emerging of things that we could do:

1. Contact bank manager **Dad**
2. Contact local newspapers and invite them to come up and look at Silverbrook Farm **Mum**
3. Find appealing animal stories on line to give examples **Me and Josh**
4. Make a leaflet for distribution door to door **Josh**
5. Arrange meeting in village hall to tell everyone the idea but also the problems. Invite newspapers and bank manager **Mum**

'A step at a time,' said Dad.
'Rome wasn't built in a day,' said Mum.

'And nor will Silverbrook be,' I said, 'but we will get there.'

'No one could say we didn't try after this,' said Mum as she looked at her watch. 'Heavens, Amy, it's eleven o'clock. Bed.'

I went up to my room feeling a million times better than I had earlier. Project Silverbrook was back on!

Chapter Ten

Cluck Cluck

'What time is le kick-off?' asked Caitlin.

I laughed. 'It's not a football match, Caitlin,' I said. 'We open the doors in five minutes, but shut the doors when people are in so Shimmer doesn't get out.'

Caitlin punched the air then did a spin. 'Yay. Get ready to rock.'

We were at the village hall on the first Saturday evening in May for a meeting with the locals. Josh, Caitlin, Shimmer and I had been there since six-thirty and Caitlin and I had set out chairs for a hundred people while Shimmer ran around sniffing in all the new scents.

The plan was to let everyone in the village know about our centre and hopefully get some of them on the bandwagon. The Westall family had gone into positive mode in the last couple of weeks and Dad had submitted his business plan to the bank. He had worked out costings with his accountant and Mum had designed plans for the café and shop with an architect. Josh had been busy with designs for the logo. All we needed now was the financing and a team of volunteers to get things started. I. Was. So. Excited.

The hall was a bit shabby. It had threadbare red velvet curtains, one of which was hanging off the pole at the windows. There was an old piano in the corner near the stage and the whole place felt cold. I wished we'd had more time to make it look cosier and get rid of the musty smell of onion soup that lingered from the pensioners' lunch earlier in the day.

We'd decided that Mum would be our spokesperson because she looked professional and wasn't shy of public speaking like Dad. He and Mum had arrived soon after us with papers, posters and leaflets for people to take away. Josh had come up with a gorgeous-looking logo for Silverbrook products, which he'd used as a header on all the leaflets. It was an ink sketch of the front of the farmhouse with roses growing over the trellis. It looked perfect. Rural but classy.

Mum had put a suit and her heels on for the occasion and looked every inch the modern businesswoman. Dad got busy setting up a table at the back of the hall showing plans for the layout of the shop, centre and café.

At half past seven, Dad gave me the thumbs up and Caitlin and I opened the door to find Mrs Watson outside.

I looked up and down the road.

No sign of anyone else.

'Where is everybody?' I asked as she came in. Mrs Watson shrugged. 'There's a big football match on tonight. Everyone will be in watching that. Me, I don't go for all that kicking a ball about. I like the soaps.'

'It can't be that,' said Mum after Mrs Watson had gone in. 'Surely not?'

Ten minutes later, Mr and Mrs O'Neill arrived with Zack and Joe. Zack gave me the thumbs up and winked. Caitlin had told me he had a crush on me. *As if.* I stuck my tongue out at him. It didn't seem to put him off because he grinned back at me.

A trickle more people arrived but, at eight o'clock, there were only seven people in the chairs.

'Should I start or not?' Mum asked.

'Give it a bit longer,' Dad said.

'Maybe Caitlin could get up and show us her acting skills,' I suggested. I was joking, but Caitlin agreed straight away.

'I could sing if you like,' she said.

'What? Old MacDonald's Farm?' I asked.

'I could do that one if you like,' said Caitlin. 'Only I could change the words to Old MacWestall's Farm. We could get people to join in.' She began to sing. '*With a woof woof here, a meow meow there …*'

Josh rolled his eyes. 'Look, why don't we do something useful? Go and talk to the people that are here so that they don't get bored. Go and explain what our plans are.'

Caitlin pouted. 'You don't think I could do it, do you, Josh?'

Josh went slightly red. 'Caitlin, I think you could do anything you set your mind to.'

Caitlin gave him a direct and meaningful look. Haha. He turned even redder.

By nine o'clock, only a couple more people had turned up. Mum and Dad went round and talked to everyone individually and gave them tea and biscuits, then they went off into the night.

'That didn't go too well, did it?' said Dad after the last one had gone.

'Happening event of the year – not,' I said.

'So what's the feedback of the people who came?' asked Mum.

Dad sighed. 'Those that came were encouraging,

glad we're doing it etc., etc. But no one offered to help,' he said.

Mum look disappointed. 'So we're back to square one,' she said.

'No,' I said. 'We keep on trying.'

'OK,' said Mum, 'but what?'

I hadn't got any ideas. Neither did Josh, Caitlin or Dad. 'I'll ask my guru,' I said.

'Guru?' asked Caitlin. 'Like an Indian man?'

'No, my business guru. My friend Natalia in Bristol. She's a fellow Silverbrook Girl – just like you.'

When I got home, I Skyped Natalia. It was lovely as always to see her smiling face on my screen. She'd had her dark curly hair braided into corn plaits since we last Skyped; it made her look cooler than ever. I used to feel so uninteresting next to her sometimes, her with her coffee-coloured glowing skin and wild hair, me with my pale face and straight, brown hair. She listened as I told her about the evening.

'So what do you think?' I asked. 'What did we do wrong?'

'You leafleted the area, you say?'

I nodded. 'Most of it.'

'Is there a posh area?'

'Yes. There are some houses down by the coast but

I don't think we could get in, they have electronic gates or long driveways.'

'They still get post, so will have letterboxes,' said Natalia. 'Try again but this time, try and organise something less boring. And always check what else is happening on the day of your event, like a football match or something else going on in the area. That's rule number one. And you have to attract people in. Hold a party. A concert. Something to make them want to come. Do you have any celebrities in the area? Sports celebrities or rock stars? Actors?'

'Oh. Don't know.'

'I'll try and find out for you. I bet there are. They buy country homes. I've read it in *Hello* magazine. Or … hold on, brain's in gear now, on a roll. How about you have a themed event? Everyone dresses up as an animal? Or vegetable.'

'No way am I going to dress up as a bit of broccoli, not even for a greater cause.'

'Fun, Amy,' said Natalia. 'You have to make it fun. A time for people to remember. A sad night out at the village hall with tea and biscuits is hardly going to stay in anyone's mind for long. You have to make an impression. Get people talking. Get creative, Silverbrook Girl.'

*

Two weeks later, I was back at the village hall dressed as a chicken. Cluck cluck. It was hard to adopt a go-getting attitude while wearing flat rubber chicken feet, a plastic beak stuck to my head and big feather trousers that made my bottom look *enormous*.

Everyone looked hilarious. After my Skype call with Natalia, we all took on board what she'd said and decided to go for the animal theme because it seemed in keeping with what we were trying to do. I'd been so worried that la famille Westall was going to spiral back into the Temple of Doom. But no. We'd been there, done that and everyone was up for moving on and trying again.

There was no fancy dress shop in our area, so we were limited to what we could buy on the internet. That didn't stop us. We ordered costumes and they arrived in the post. Mum was dressed as a scary rabbit with big teeth and hands with claws. Josh was a dog. Mr O'Neill was a bull and Mrs O'Neill came dressed as a sweet white bunny. She is the spitting image of Caitlin, only older and chubbier. She looked very pretty in her outfit. Her and Mum made a funny-looking pair, good bunny and bad bunny. Zack was a shark and Joe a turtle. Not to leave Shimmer out, I'd put a pair of deer's antlers on her. She looked so cute. Caitlin was a tigress in a skin-tight outfit which she wore with high black boots. She looked amazing, and even Josh gave her a second look when she came in. Dad was dressed as a gorilla even though we'd told him that you don't often find gorillas – or tigers, in Caitlin's case – in Somerset and the chance of anyone bringing them to our rescue centre was unlikely. But they were the only costumes. It didn't matter, though – dressing up put everyone in a really good mood.

Mum and Mrs O'Neill had become friends in the last few weeks and had bonded over baking. They'd spent hours making cakes and jam to show what sorts of things the shop could sell. Mum was so excited at the idea of running her own shop and seemed to love making things that could go in it. She was good at it too. Her carrot cake with lemon icing and date and walnut cakes were amazing. Her enthusiasm for cooking seemed to have won Mrs Watson round, and she wasn't treating us so much like 'the outsiders' any more. Even she had made an effort for today and was wearing a Winnie the Pooh hat over her white hair.

We'd hired the hall for the day and had been there since early morning. We decorated with balloons and anything we could find to make it look more party-like. Mrs O'Neill had brought a plastic blow-up palm tree from when they had a jungle themed party for Joe's last birthday. Caitlin and I brought all our old soft toys and lined them up at the front of the stage. We had teddies, rabbits, monkeys, a polar bear, Mickey Mouse and a few Little Ponies from when I was really little. I was glad I hadn't thrown them away when I'd grown out of them. It was like seeing old friends up there on the stage. Dad brought all our Christmas lights and hung them from the corners of the hall. It all looked a bit mad seeing it was May and a sunny day outside, but it was colourful and made the hall look like a special occasion was going to take place.

At the back, Mr O'Neill had set out baskets of his products from his paddocks. I gave him the thumbs up.

'I like your costume,' he said.

'Cluck, cluck,' I replied and did a wiggle. 'Everyone's going to be wearing outfits like this soon. I'm a trend-setter don't you know?'

'I'm sure it will catch on,' he said with a perfectly straight face.

Josh had done some new leaflets with the help of Natalia on the other end of the computer.

They said:

A SPECIAL invitation to the PARTY of the year
Time: Saturday 17th May 2.30pm – 5pm
Place: The village hall in Compton Truit
Reason: To celebrate the beginning of a new
venture coming soon –
Silverbrook Farm café, shop and animal
rescue centre
Dress: Casual or animal
Everyone welcome
Don't miss it!

We'd leafleted the area again last weekend, including the part near the coast with the posh-looking houses. I found it intimidating going up to some of them, especially the Tudor mansion, where we saw Poppy Pengilly. She gave us a funny look when she saw us, but I did my best to ignore it and smiled at her. I loved the way she dressed in riders' gear – a fitted jacket, jodhpurs and high leather boots. She was clearly a horsey person. That was a good sign.

We shoved Josh forward to give her a leaflet and it appeared he worked his usual charm because she took one and chatted to him for a while. Her dad came out to ask who we were and Poppy gave him the leaflet, which he didn't even look at. He just shoved it in his pocket and politely showed us back to the gate.

'Her name's Poppy,' said Josh when we got outside the grounds. 'Poppy Pengilly.' He seemed slightly awestruck.

'We know,' I said. 'She goes to our school.'

'Her crowd are very snooty,' said Caitlin. I think she was jealous.

Sadly we couldn't find any celebrities in the area, although there was a rumour that the soap actor Tyrrel Turner lived somewhere around. No one knew exactly where, but Natalia said she'd try and find out.

At two-twenty-five, I looped Shimmer's lead around a chair so that she didn't go mad when people arrived, then we plugged Josh's iPod into the sound system. Josh had made a special playlist of all the songs he could find about animals from songs from *Jungle Book*, and *Dr Doolittle* to 'Puff the Magic Dragon' and 'Crocodile Rock'.

Caitlin was on door duty to let people in and, as soon as she opened them, people began to stream in. Parents came with children dressed as penguins, zebras, kangaroos, monsters, elephants, whales, deer and one cute little hamster. It appeared that everyone welcomed a chance to dress up in Compton Truit.

The atmosphere was so different to our first meeting in the hall and was soon buzzing as people laughed at each other's costumes and got chatting, some people even danced along to the music. Mum and Mrs O'Neill ran out of cakes after an hour and were doing a roaring trade on their homemade chutneys. Mrs Watson was busy making teas and Mr O'Neill's fruit and veg were disappearing fast too.

I nudged Caitlin to look over at Shimmer, who was sitting by her chair, her tail wagging happily as a boy with sandy hair and a sweet face made a fuss of her. He wasn't the first. She'd been having a great afternoon as the centre of attention – as soon as anyone saw her, they'd go over to give her a stroke. She'd sat there loving it all. The boy who was with her was dressed as a chimp and was joined by another boy who wasn't in costume and was dressed in a black T-shirt and jeans. I recognised him straight away. It was Liam, the boy we'd met by the river. He and the younger boy looked like brothers, although Liam had a sullen look about him as if he didn't want to be in the hall at all. I wondered why he'd come, then I saw Mrs Watson call them over.

'They might be her nephews,' I said. 'I heard her talking about them one day in the tea shop. I think the younger one is about ten and is called Robbie.'

'It's a shame Liam is so grumpy,' said Caitlin, 'he looks like he's eaten a wasp.'

Caitlin giggled as Liam glanced over at us and I smiled. He didn't smile back so I looked away to show I didn't care. I didn't. I could see a couple of elderly ladies talking to Mum so I went to eavesdrop.

'I think it would be marvellous if you set up your centre,' said one of the ladies who was very well-spoken and dressed in a smart lavender-coloured suit and pearls. 'I worry what will become of my cats if anything happens to me. I'm almost ninety you know. I can't live forever and I have no family left to step in and give them a home.'

Mum assured her that her cats would be well looked after if she had anything to do with it, then went and got chairs for both ladies and gave them a free piece of cake and cup of tea.

'Maybe you'd like to come and visit one day,' said the well-spoken lady. 'You could meet my cats, Millie and Myrtle. They're darlings.'

'I'd love to,' said Mum and the old lady got out a notepad from her handbag and gave Mum her address. It sounded very grand. She was Mrs Carter-West of Lymington House.

On the far side of the hall, I saw that Poppy Pengilly had come in with her father. They weren't dressed up as animals and walked around like they were royalty, looking down their noses at everything and everybody.

Poppy pointed to the plastic palm tree, said something to her dad that I couldn't hear and they both laughed. *Stuck up princess*, I thought. I saw them nod hello to Mrs Carter-West then go to look at the vegetable stalls. I also noticed Liam scowling at them as they walked around. They didn't buy anything and didn't stay long.

After they'd gone, I saw a man talking to Dad then he got out a recording device. I waddled over (it was hard to walk properly in my rubber feet) to hear what was going on. He was from the local radio station. *Excellent*, I thought as Dad filled him in. Mum had contacted them with an invitation the week before but we hadn't heard back, so weren't sure that they'd come. She'd also contacted the local paper, but I didn't know if they'd turned up, though it was hard to tell who was who because some of the adults were in costume and others busy with their kids. Caitlin was leading a small group of under-fives in a rousing chorus of 'Old MacWestall's Farm'. She'd finally got to do it. I giggled at how out of place she looked as a tiger, but when she sang, 'Old MacWestall had a tiger, ee i ee i o,' they all joined in with gusto.

Around three-thirty, Mum went up on to the stage and called for everyone's attention. When the hall was silent, she began to explain what we wanted to do at

Silverbrook Farm. She was still dressed in her scary bunny costume.

'Do you think people will take her seriously?' I asked Caitlin. 'Maybe she should have changed back into her businesswoman clothes.'

Caitlin shook her head. 'Nah. People love it. Look, everyone's listening and the outfit lets them know that she's a fun person and up for whatever it takes to make things work.'

'It will take us a while to get up and running,' Mum was saying, 'but we hope that we'll be a welcome addition to the community here in Compton Truit. We want to sell only local produce in the shop and café so we will be looking for suppliers of meat, bread, fruit, homemade cakes, jams, juice — whatever you think you or a neighbour could make and we could sell — we could put local artists' paintings on the wall … we're open to all ideas. And hopefully the rest of you will come and use the café and shop. We'll also be looking for volunteers when we have the rescue centre set up. If you have any skills that you think might be helpful, please make yourself known to us and leave your details.'

'How long do you think it will take to get set up?' asked one man, who was with a little boy dressed as a zebra.

'Good question,' Mum replied. 'That all depends on the response from the community. We hope to have the shop and café going first and, once they're open, we can put our energy into establishing the rescue centre. But all in all, we want to create a place that will provide employment for some, a place to meet for others, somewhere for visitors to come and see the best that the village has to offer.'

When she'd finished, people cheered. I felt so proud of her even if she did look like she'd just walked off the set of a scary cartoon.

When everyone had gone, we totted up the profits. We'd made two hundred and forty-three pounds.

'OK, so not thousands,' said Dad, 'but today wasn't about raising lots of money. It was about raising interest – and I think we accomplished that. I already have a list of people who would like to make things to sell at the shop. Everyone is very enthusiastic. One farmer said he could supply meat and would speak to other farmers in the area. Most people said that they'd spread the word – I think today has been a real success!'

It was then that I noticed that Shimmer wasn't around. 'Shimmer … Dad, where's Shimmer?'

Everyone looked around, but there was no sign of her.

'When did you last see her?' asked Mum.

'Not long ago. She was here a moment ago. I'm sure she was! Maybe she's in one of the back rooms, you know how she loves sniffing around new areas,' I said and raced off to search the hall, my heart thumping in my chest.

Everyone started searching the building, calling her name, but she didn't come.

I felt a rising panic. I couldn't bear it if anything had happened to her.

Caitlin came and put her arm around me. 'She must have wandered out when people left. She can't be far.'

'But I tied her lead to a chair,' I said, panicking more now. 'She couldn't have got out unless she dragged the chair with her — and we'd have heard that.' Tears sprang to my eyes as I imagined how scared she would be if she'd got lost.

'And we kept the doors shut after people arrived,' said Josh. 'I've kept an eye on it all afternoon and made sure it was closed and only open to let people leave.'

I raced to the doors and out on to the pavement, where I looked up and down the road. There was no sign of her. She had definitely gone.

Chapter Eleven

Looking for Shimmer

'Let's split up,' said Dad. 'Josh, you take the left on foot, Caitlin and Amy, you go right. I'll get in the car and drive up and down the streets.' He turned to Mr O'Neill. 'Maybe you could drive around too, Mike. I'll go north, you go south.'

'I'm on it,' said Mr O'Neill, heading off to his car. 'Don't worry, Amy, we'll find her.'

Mum pointed at Mrs O'Neill. 'Shannon and I will stay here and clear up and see if Shimmer comes back, or anyone finds her. She might have just wandered off somewhere. Everyone got their phones?'

Caitlin, Josh and I nodded.

'I'll be base camp,' Mum continued. 'Call me if there's any news.'

Everyone shot off in the direction Dad had directed

them. I felt breathless and close to tears as we ran up and down the road, looking in front gardens, peering over fences and calling Shimmer's name. 'I can't bear it if anything's happened to her,' I said. 'It's my fault, I should have been keeping a closer eye on her!'

'Don't worry, we'll find her,' said Caitlin. 'SHIMMER! Where are you?'

'I can't believe she'd have gone off on her own. She never likes to be far away from me. I honestly don't understand what could have happened. Her lead was tied to the chair. Do you think it came loose? Or … oh Caitlin, do you think someone might have stolen her? She is so beautiful.'

Caitlin squeezed my arm. 'We'll find her. It had crossed my mind that someone might have taken her – but this is a small village, it would get out if someone had her. Someone would notice.'

As we ran along the road, we saw a man who had been at the hall. 'Excuse me, have you seen my dog?' I asked. 'She's a golden retriever.'

'I saw one in the village hall but not since,' he replied. 'Why, have you lost her?'

I nodded. 'We looked around and she'd gone.'

The man shook his head then rolled his eyes. His face had a pinched look and his hair looked as though it needed a good wash. 'You're the people who want to run the animal rescue centre, aren't you?' he said. 'And you can't even keep track of your own dog? Not a good start that, is it?'

Caitlin pulled me away. 'That's not very helpful, Mr …'

'Mr Braithwaite,' said the man. 'Best of luck.' He turned and went into a terraced house nearby.

'He didn't sound like he meant that,' said Caitlin as he disappeared inside.

We spent another half an hour searching the streets. We got some very odd looks because I was still in my chicken outfit and Caitlin was still dressed as a tiger. At first people laughed when we said we were looking for a dog, but they stopped when they saw we were genuinely worried. No one had seen her.

I stopped a lady at the bus stop. 'You haven't seen a dog on its own, have you?' I asked.

'Yes, I have. About fifteen minutes ago. Ran by here.'

'Where? Which way did she go? Was she on her own?' I could have wept with relief – I'd been imagining someone stealing her and driving her away from the area.

'Oh it wasn't a she,' said the lady.

'How do you know?' asked Caitlin.

'It was a boy. A teenager.'

'With the dog?' I asked. I felt confused.

'No. *Dressed* as a dog. He had on a costume.'

'Josh,' said Caitlin, exasperatedly. 'She saw Josh. Sorry, we're not looking for someone dressed as a dog, we're looking for an actual dog. A white–golden retriever. We've lost her.'

The bus came round the corner and the lady put her hand out. 'In that case, I can't help. Sorry.' As the bus opened its door, she stepped on. Everyone on the bus was staring and pointing at us. I felt close to tears again. My imagination was running wild. What if Shimmer had run into traffic? What if she was hurt?

At that moment, my phone rang. It was Mum.

'Amy, come back. Dad and Mr O'Neill said that they can cover more ground in the car.'

'So they haven't found her?'

'Not yet.'

I felt my heart sink further. 'Can I go with Dad?'

'Why don't you come back to the hall and we'll go home and wait for news there.'

'Please let me go with Dad,' I pleaded. 'I'll go mad waiting at home. Please let me do something, Mum.'

I knew I couldn't rest until we found her.

When it got dark, Dad gave up the search and drove home, though I begged him to stay out looking for Shimmer. 'We can use our energy other ways,' he said.

'Posters, phone calls – we're not giving up by going home, Amy, just changing the way we search.'

When we got back to the house, we saw that Josh had already been busy and was printing out posters to put on lampposts and trees. 'I wanted to go straight out and put them up, but Mum wouldn't let me,' he said.

'No one's going to see them in the dark,' Mum said gently. 'Have some supper, get a good night's sleep and we'll start again in the morning. She can't have got far and tomorrow we can go door to door asking if anyone has seen her. It's a small village. News travels fast.'

Caitlin had said something similar, but it didn't make me feel any better. I couldn't eat a thing, didn't sleep a wink and had a horrible night. How could I sleep or eat when Shimmer might be somewhere strange, hungry and wondering where I was – or, even worse, hurt by a roadside? *We should have stayed out looking*, I thought as I tossed and turned in my bed.

I was up early on Sunday morning and once again Mum tried to get me to eat something, but I couldn't. I felt sick with worry and my stomach churned again as my imagination played images in my mind of what might have happened to Shimmer.

Dad drove Josh and me into the village where we

got busy putting up posters on trees and walls. Mum stayed at home at 'base camp' again, to be there if anyone phoned with news.

A few villagers stopped and asked about the posters, but no one had seen or heard of Shimmer. I felt so empty and sad, like a part of me was missing. In the weeks I'd had Shimmer, I'd grown to love her and her funny ways – her enthusiasm (Mum would say greed) for food and how she'd eat like she'd never had a meal before. Two gulps and it was gone, then she'd get the hiccups and, all the time, she'd look as if she was smiling. If any of us forgot her suppertime, she'd come and stand next to one of us and nudge us until we fed her. The way she hated salad always made me laugh and her look of disdain if we offered her a carrot or piece of cucumber was hilarious. Any dog toy we give her would last four minutes max, but somehow she knew not to touch my old soft toys that were on the shelf behind my bed. I wonder how she knew that they weren't for chewing? She was so cute, had a pure heart, loved me unconditionally and was always in a good mood. She was so lovely and soft to snuggle up with after school, she'd nestle her head under my chin and settle down like she knew she belonged. She was one of the family – and to think about life without her was unimaginable. Last night, the house felt so quiet without her in it. She made everyone in our family smile and there was no doubt that we were all happier for having had her come into our lives.

After a couple of hours, I sat on the pavement and cried.

Dad was about to sit next to me when his phone rang. Josh and I watched and listened to his end of the conversation expectantly. *Please, please let someone have found her*, I prayed as I stood back up.

Dad shook his head after the call. 'It was just Mike asking if there'd been any news and saying that he and Caitlin will come and help out if we need.'

I sank back down on to the pavement. 'What could they do? I am the most useless person in the world,' I said. 'I don't deserve to have such a beautiful dog if I can't look after her. It's all my fault, if I'd been watching over her more, this wouldn't have happened and now you'll never let me keep her.'

'Amy, it's not over yet,' said Dad. 'And you mustn't blame yourself. You tied her lead to a chair. You didn't just abandon her. She's not even been gone a day yet. Give it time. Dogs don't just disappear into thin air. She has to be somewhere.'

'But what do we do now?' I asked.

Dad shrugged. 'I don't know. We wait, I guess. Someone is bound to have seen something. When people see the posters, they'll start talking. Someone *must* have seen something.'

We got into the car to go back home and Dad's mobile rang again. As Dad took the call, I held my breath, hardly daring to hope.

Chapter Twelve

Unexpected Volunteers

As Dad listened, I saw his expression lighten; he glanced over at me and gave me the thumbs up. He clicked off the phone.

'That was Mum. Shimmer's been found.'

I let out a breath of air. Tears came into my eyes again, this time with relief. 'Where was she? Is she OK?'

'She's fine. Apparently Mrs Watson brought her back.'

'Mrs Watson?' asked Josh.

Dad nodded. 'Seems one of her nephews took Shimmer and hid him in her garden shed.' Dad frowned as he was saying this. 'She's taking her back to the house now.'

I bet it was Liam, I thought as we headed for home.

He probably thought it was funny. Poppy warned me about him. I am so going to kill him.

When we got home, Shimmer was back already and scoffing down a big bowl of food. She went mad when she saw me and rushed towards me with the same excitement I felt at seeing her again.

I knelt down and she leaped on to my knees, put her paws on my shoulders and gave my face a very enthusiastic licking. 'Pleased to see you too, Shimmer. I don't think I will ever need to wash my face again!' I said as I wrapped my arms around her soft wriggling body. 'And I will never let you go again.'

Shimmer wagged her tail as if agreeing.

'She's fine,' said Mum. 'And she's just eaten two bowls of food.'

'That nasty Liam. Why did he take her?' I said.

Mum looked puzzled. 'Mrs Watson didn't mention Liam. No, she said it was the younger one who took Shimmer – Robbie.'

'Robbie? But why?'

'I'm not sure. Maybe he couldn't resist her. I've heard theirs is not a happy home so we should try to be sympathetic. Mrs Watson was very apologetic, but begged us not to be too angry with him. Apparently his dad is hard enough. She's going to bring Robbie up later to apologise in person, but has asked that we don't complain to his father. She said if he found out, he might make Robbie's life a misery, more than it is already.' I thought about how much I loved Shimmer, and how upset I was that she'd been taken. But I also remembered how much happiness she'd brought to our family and I understood, just a tiny bit, why Robbie might have wanted to take her for himself, especially if he was unhappy at home.

Later that day, I was playing ball with Shimmer in the yard when Mrs Watson's car drove up, with her and Robbie inside. She stopped at the front and I could see she was saying something to Robbie, who was in the passenger seat. They both got out and, when Mrs Watson saw me, she came towards me. Mum and Dad must have heard her car arrive because they came out to greet her.

Robbie stayed close to the car and stood looking at his feet. His eyes were swollen and I could see that he'd been crying.

'Come on, Robbie, what have you got to say to the Westalls?' asked Mrs Watson.

Robbie shifted about, but still didn't look up. When Shimmer saw him, she ran up to him and put her paws up to his knees, her tail wagging. She was clearly pleased to see him.

Robbie looked bewildered, as if he didn't know what to do. Shimmer gave him an encouraging bark to say, '*Oi, don't ignore me.*' Finally Robbie looked up and his expression broke my heart. He looked so worried. 'I … am … *so* … sorry I took your dog, Amy,' he stuttered. 'I didn't mean any harm. Just she's so cute, I only meant to take her for a walk and play with her a bit and then … and …'

I could see that he was genuinely sorry so I went over and put my arm around him. 'Do you promise to never steal her again?'

He looked up at me and I tried to look back as kindly as I could.

'No. I won't,' he said. 'I mean – I won't steal her, not that I won't promise.'

Shimmer was still pawing at his knees, desperate for attention, so he bent down and stroked her and she licked his hand. 'She's the cutest dog I've ever seen,' he said. 'I wouldn't have harmed her.'

'But you do know it's wrong to take a dog that doesn't belong to you,' said Dad.

Robbie's eyes grew huge with alarm. He swallowed nervously then nodded. 'I do. I won't do it again, promise and … and … my aunt says you want volunteers to work on your centre. I volunteer. I'll do anything.' He glanced over at one of the open stables.

'I love animals, me. I'll come and live here if you like. I'm a good washer-upper and a fast learner.'

Dad smiled. 'That won't be necessary, son,' he said, 'but your help would be welcome when we're up and running.'

Robbie's face broke into a grin. 'Honest?'

'In the meantime, do you want to play with Shimmer and me?' I asked. I remembered Shimmer when she first came to Silverbrook. She'd looked so confused and just wanted someone to be kind to her. Robbie had that same sad look in his eyes. Plus it might be fun to have a boy around that wasn't Josh.

Robbie's eyes grew large again, like they were going to pop out of his head. 'Could I?'

I nodded. 'She loves chasing a tennis ball.' I handed him a ball and he was off, throwing, with Shimmer scampering after him.

Mum came and put her arm around me and gave me a squeeze. 'Good girl, Amy. That was generous of you.'

I squeezed her back. 'He seems sad,' I said. 'I couldn't be angry with him for long.'

Mum looked over to where Robbie was playing with Shimmer. 'I know what you mean.'

Chapter Thirteen

Disaster

'Have you seen this?'

I'd just got home with Dad, who'd picked me up from school on Wednesday afternoon. He was in a good mood because he'd had news. The bank was going to give him a loan and it would be enough to start the work converting the stables into a shop and café. All the way home, he'd added whistling to his usual tuneless humming. I joined in for a while. Hmm, hmm, hmm, whistle, whistle, dum de dah da.

'Seen what?' Dad asked Mum.

She handed him a copy of the local paper. 'It's a disaster,' she said. Dad took it, read it then sighed.

'What? What is it?' I asked. I picked up the paper and read for myself. 'Oh *no*.'

ANIMAL RESCUE CENTRE FAILS BEFORE IT HAS BEGUN, said the headline.

After an animal themed afternoon on Saturday 17th May, the Westall family managed to lose their first animal resident, Shimmer. A search party was sent out but to no avail. 'I looked around and she was gone,' said Amy Westall (11) after the event had ended.

Newcomers to the area, the Westalls, spoke about plans to offer employment for locals and a shelter for lost pets. However, after managing to lose their first puppy, it makes this local wonder if they can be trusted to deliver on any of their promises and if maybe it was all hot air.

I looked to see who had written it. Nathan Braithwaite, it said.

'I know who he is. He's the man Caitlin and I bumped into when we were out looking for Shimmer,' I said. 'He said then he wasn't impressed.'

'But it wasn't our fault,' said Mum. 'It's very unfair of him not to get the facts. Someone should set him straight.'

'We can't do that, love. We can't tell him what really happened,' said Dad. 'We promised Mrs Watson that we wouldn't say anything about Robbie and now I've met him, I'm inclined to agree. I don't want the boy getting into trouble. Sadly, Mr Nathan Braithwaite has got us over a barrel. We can't go back to him and defend ourselves without naming names – but I agree, it seems very unfair.' He sighed again. 'Just as we'd won over the locals, they'll see something like this.'

'So what can we do? What if anyone asks?' I asked.

'Josh's already taken down all the posters we put up around the village. If anyone asks, we say Shimmer wasn't lost. We say it was a case of miscommunication and a friend was looking after her all the time,' said Dad.

'Sounds fishy to me,' said Mum. 'But I don't think we have any choice. We can't land Robbie in it. We'll just have to prove Mr Braithwaite wrong, that's all. We have to show him that Shimmer is the most obedient, well-behaved and well-looked-after dog that ever lived.'

Josh came in to join us. 'And I can keep putting stuff on our Facebook page to show that Shimmer's home and safe. It's all set up now.'

'I know what else we can do,' I said. 'I've seen it on other doggie pages online. On days like Christmas, they put tinsel on their dogs; on St Patrick's, a green hat; and things like that. One lady even put heart-shaped glasses on her dog on Valentine's Day. They look *so* cute. At least it will show Shimmer is well and happy, and each festival or diary date is an excuse to show an update of her and what's happening here.'

'And if we do some basic training with her,' said Dad, 'we can put some photos of that up. Show that we are responsible. Good idea, Amy. That's what we need to keep doing, posting stuff so that Mr Braithwaite's article becomes yesterday's news.'

'So, Shimmer, are you ready for your training sessions?' I looked over at Shimmer, who was at that moment chewing one of Dad's shoes. Luckily it was one of an old pair. 'Hmm, I reckon we might have a challenge on there. OK. Shimmer, come here, girl.'

Shimmer looked at me then back at the shoe. She rolled on her back and carried on chewing the shoe. I got up and went over to her. 'Drop,' I commanded. 'Drop shoe.'

Shimmer thought it was a game. She got the shoe firmly in her mouth and went and hid under the table where I couldn't get at her. I followed her over. 'Shimmer, drop. Drop the shoe.'

She ran out into the hall, still with the shoe in her mouth, and hid under the hall table, her tail wagging. She was good at this game. Next she ran up the stairs. I followed her up to see she'd hidden under my bed.

She was peeking out, the shoe firmly under her front paws.

There had to be another way.

I went to my laptop and Googled 'how to train your dog'.

I sat at my computer for hours. I watched videos on YouTube. I read websites with top tips. I made notes. I watched training sessions on how to get a dog to sit, stand, roll, stop on command. All the time, Shimmer lay at my feet happily chewing on Dad's shoe.

'Haha, Shim my girl, you don't know what you're in for!' I said.

The next evening, I took Shimmer out into the yard after school. Dad, Josh and Ginger came out to watch. I started with practising commands to sit. As always, Shimmer thought it was a game and started running around and jumping up with excitement at all the attention she was getting. Ginger sat on one of the bins and surveyed the scene with his usual look of disdain.

'Sit,' said Josh. 'Sit.'

'I know you're trying to help, Josh, but according to what I read, it will be confusing for her if she hears commands from different people. She won't know who to listen to. It's important that I establish myself

as the main pack leader or else Shimmer will get confused. They like to know who's their boss — it makes
them feel safe and secure.'

'Ooh. All hail the mighty Amy,' said Josh.

'She's right, Josh,' said Dad. 'Dogs are pack animals.
All domesticated dogs are descended from wolves and
their basic instinct tells them that there has to be a
hierarchy and one leader.'

Josh shrugged. 'OK, but don't think you get to be
leader of the whole family.'

'As if,' I said. 'We all know who that is.'

'Mum,' we chorused.

Dad laughed. 'And that's a fact,' he said, looking over
at Ginger. 'With Ginger second in command.'

Ginger blinked his eyes slowly as if agreeing.

When Dad and Josh went back inside, I turned back
to Shimmer. 'We both get homework now,' I told her.
'And we'll show the villagers. You're going to be
Shimmer the Wonder Dog.'

The first few sessions were hopeless. I gave the command to sit. Shimmer rolled on her back. I gave the
command to roll over. She sat. Then she'd bark. As the
YouTube demonstrations had advised, I turned my
back on her when she did that and only when she'd
stopped did I turn back, kneel down, look into her

eyes and firmly say, '*No*'. She put her paws on my shoulders and gave me a good licking.

'Yes, I like you too, Shimmer, but you have to learn some basic commands.' She got down, then turned back and jumped up with such enthusiasm that I went flying on to my back. As I was lying sprawled out on the yard, I heard a male voice. 'Need a hand?'

I looked up. It was Liam. Robbie's sulky brother. I scrambled to my feet. 'No. I'm fine. I ... I'm just training my dog.'

Liam cracked up laughing. 'Yeah. Looks like you're winning too.'

'No need to be sarcastic,' I said. 'It's early days.'

'Very early,' said Liam. His face had resumed its normal sour expression.

'What do you want?' I asked.

'My aunt sent me up to say me and Robbie have to come on Saturdays to help out.'

'*Have* to come? Robbie seemed very happy about it.'

For a second, Liam's mean mask disappeared and he looked worried. 'You're not going to say anything about Rob, are you? About him taking your dog?'

I shook my head. 'No. We like him.'

Liam looked relieved and his face softened. 'He's a good kid. Loves animals. Mad about them. And ... our dad ...' He didn't finish the sentence.

'What about your mum?' I asked.

'We don't have a mum. She died just after Robbie was born.'

'Oh I'm sorry,' I said. 'I didn't know.'

His sullen mask was back in a flash. 'We don't need you to feel sorry for us. Just don't tell Dad about Robbie taking your dog.' He looked around. 'Anyway, we'll be here Saturday morning.'

'OK, I'll tell Mum,' I said. 'Would you …' I was going to make an effort to be more friendly and offer him a glass of juice, but he'd already turned away and was trudging back down the lane. Whatever else was going on his life, he certainly had a soft spot for his younger brother.

Chapter Fourteen

Shimmer the Welly Wee-er

Dear Diary,

Shimmer's training:

Day One: when we were out walking in the park down by the river, a lady stopped, put her handbag down and leaned over to say hello to Shimmer, who greeted her back by weeing on her wellies. So embarrassing. I knelt down, looked into Shimmer's eyes and said, 'No,' very firmly. I hope she got the message. The lady gave me a stern lecture about how to control my dog. While I was listening to her, Shimmer went behind her and weed on her handbag. Oops. Luckily, the lady didn't notice and hopefully, it dried out by the time she got home.

Day Two: Robbie came out for a walk with

Shimmer and me. I explained the rules to him. We acted very pleased when Shimmer weed on a tree by making a big fuss of her, giving her a little dog treat and saying, 'Yes, good girl.' Also acted not pleased when she weed on a lamppost. I said, 'No,' in a firm voice. Shimmer just looked confused. How does one explain the difference between a tree and a lamppost to a dog? I asked Robbie. He didn't have an answer, though he tried to explain whilst pointing at the tree and then the lamppost, but Shimmer just wagged her tail because she was getting more attention. Robbie couldn't stop laughing and, in the end, Shimmer seemed to find it funny too and started running around chasing her tail to show she had other tricks she could do besides weeing.

Day Three: Ew. No one told me that dogs can poo for Britain, and Shimmer is a champion at it. As I was scooping up her latest into a poo bag whilst holding my nose, the snooty girls from my school, including Poppy Pengilly, went past and stared at me. 'Dog poo,' I called to them, by way of explanation. They looked at me as if I was mad – I think they thought I was calling them dog poo. As if. I only call Natalia names like that. Or Josh. One of them called back, 'Dog poo yourself.' I think they think I'm totally lame. I did wonder about getting Shimmer to

wee on their shoes, but resisted despite the temptation.
Revenge of the Weeing Dog. Yeah, watch out, girls of
Compton Truit. I have a furry weapon and her name
is Shimmer.

Day Four: Articles chewed: pair of slippers. Books.
Kitchen table legs and chair legs. Shimmer also
decided it would be fun to take a running jump on to
the kitchen table, but was going too fast and the
surface was slippery so she skidded all the way along
it and almost fell off at the other end. Mum said,
'No,' to her in her very firm Mum-voice and
Shimmer didn't do it again. Much as I try, I think
Mum is the ultimate pack leader.

Day Five: Back to the park, this time with
Caitlin. I noticed the lady in the wellies. As soon as
she saw us, she went the other way.

When we got to the area where dogs are allowed
off their lead, I let Shimmer go and she bolted off
towards a family having a picnic with two toddlers. In
a flash, she helped herself to their sandwiches. One
gulp and they were gone (the sandwiches, not the
children). I blew the whistle Dad had given me, but
Shimmer took no notice. And I did go over and
apologise, but the couple were too busy calming their
terrified toddlers.

Once again, I knelt down, looked Shimmer in the

eyes and said, 'No.' She licked my face in response.
Ew. A tuna and mayonnaise flavoured lick. So not
what I want to smell of.

Caitlin asked if Mum or Dad had said any more
about letting me keep Shimmer. She is so happy with
Cola and Pepsi and is forever showing me photos of
them that she's taken on her phone. I wish I had the
same confidence that Shimmer was really really mine.
I replied that my plan was to be Very Well Behaved
Daughter and to train Shimmer to be Very Well
Behaved Dog then they couldn't refuse. Her question
did worry me, though, because no one has mentioned
finding Shimmer another home for ages, but that
doesn't mean they aren't thinking about it.

Day Six: Same park. This time I kept Shimmer
on a lead, but when a child eating an ice cream
walked past us, Shimmer got the scent of it. Vanilla,
her favourite. She pulled at her lead and went for it;
the girl tumbled over, dropped the ice cream and with
one suck it was gone. Oops. Apologised to her parents.
Am thinking of getting a sign printed and having it
stuck to my forehead saying I AM SORRY
ABOUT MY DOG.

Repeat of Day Five, on my knees, I say, 'No,' to
Shimmer. A big lick back – vanilla flavoured this
time.

She did make some new friends though: Bentley, Eddie and Tiger. Funny how their way of saying hi is to sniff each other's bottom. Not very ladylike in my opinion, but it seems to be the thing to do if you're a dog.

Day Seven: Out on our walk with Robbie again. He loves coming with us and is a real sweetie, plus Shimmer seems to like him too. Before I could stop her, Shimmer ate some bit of old rubbish she found on the path then got a runny tummy. On the way home, she pooed in someone's driveway. Ew. And not the kind I could put in a poo bag (double ew) so I tipped my bottle of water over it and we ran off and hid behind a bush. Robbie couldn't stop laughing again and Shimmer looked very happy to be hiding as it is one of her favourite games. I really hope no one saw us, especially Mr Braithwaite. The last thing we need is another horrible headline. Westalls' Family Pet Strikes Again. Shimmer is a very loving dog but a stubborn one, and this train-your-dog lark is not as easy as they make it look on YouTube.

After a few weeks, Shimmer seemed to be getting the hang of some of the more basic commands and responded to the whistle that Dad had given me to bring her back if ever she ran too far. I'd stuck with it and repeated and repeated her lessons, giving rewards when she was good and ignoring her or saying 'No, bad girl' when she was disobedient, and blowing the whistle so she knew where I was if she'd wandered off. In the end, she caught on and I could tell she understood my different tones of voice. Hurrah!

On the last Saturday in June, I went with Caitlin into the village for the next step in Shimmer's training, which was learning to be with other people. So far, she'd thought everyone was her friend, all food was for her and rubber boots were for peeing on. I had to get her to behave better in public.

She trotted up and down the village street and was the model of good behaviour. She didn't pull on the lead, she stopped when I told her to and she sat when I told her to. I felt so proud of her.

'Seeing as it's so hot,' Caitlin said, 'maybe we should try the beach, where you can let her off the lead.'

'OK, let's see how she gets on.'

We got the bus and, once again, Shimmer was very good and sat at my feet quietly.

'I think we're making progress,' I told Caitlin.

When we got there, the beach was packed, people were sunbathing and I noticed there were a few dogs running around and enjoying the freedom. I quickly checked to see if there were any sandwiches or ice creams around, but the coast seemed to be clear.

'OK, Shimmer,' I said as I let her off the lead. 'Now stay.' Shimmer took no notice, charged off and straight into the water, darting in and out of the waves with glee. 'She loves the sea. It's becoming her favourite thing.'

We watched for a while then Caitlin suddenly pointed. 'Oops,' she said.

Shimmer had got out of the water and run over to where a couple were snoozing in the sun, the man in a pair of shorts and the woman in her bikini. I knew what was going to happen, and there was nothing I could do. Shimmer stood right next to them … and did the doggie shake. Her outline was a blur of fur and water, and the couple leaped up as though they'd been electrocuted. If Shimmer hadn't been my dog, I would have burst out laughing, but the man started yelling at Shimmer and running after her. He looked really angry and was definitely not one to mess with.

Caitlin looked worried. 'Let's pretend she's not with us,' she said.

'It's tempting but … I have to own up,' I replied.

I was about to go forward when suddenly a boy appeared and called Shimmer to him – Liam! Shimmer recognised him and went straight to him. He reached down and held Shimmer by her collar. Although we couldn't hear, I could see by Liam's body language that he was apologising to the couple, backing away from them and almost bowing. Shimmer soon got the message and backed away too. They looked as if they were backing away from a king, both bowing their heads, and again it was hard not to laugh. The man in the shorts still looked mad though, his face red with anger. He shouted something, then Liam headed towards us and luckily the man went back to his girlfriend.

Liam handed Shimmer to me and I quickly put her back on her lead. 'See the dog training's going well then,' he said, but not in a nasty way.

'Liam, thank you so much. You took the rap for us,' I said.

Liam shrugged. 'No problem,' he said. 'I'm well used to grown-ups yelling at me … and stuck-up girls like Poppy Pengilly yelling at me too. But listen, I know that bloke, he's a mate of my dad's and believe me, you don't want to get in his bad books.' Then he grinned. 'You should have seen their faces though. Shimmer, you bad dog, you soaked them.'

Shimmer wagged her tail, delighted as always to be the centre of attention.

I sighed. 'It's not easy training a dog, you know. For a start, we're supposed to ignore her when she's been bad, not make a fuss of her.'

'Don't worry,' said Liam. 'You'll get the hang of it. Dogs are simple creatures. Ignore them when they're behaving badly, reward them when they've done something right.'

Caitlin planted a big kiss on Liam's cheek. 'And *you* just did something right,' she said.

'Be-wuhnuh,' Liam stuttered. He'd gone bright red. *So he's not always Mr Cool-as-a-cucumber,* I thought as I gave him a big hug.

Chapter Fifteen

Invasion of the Men in Suits

Dear Diary,

House: doors are open, windows are open, the sunshine is shining in, it feels like a different place to when we landed mid-winter.

Animals: the Cluckie Gang (hens) seem happy, though Shimmer does like to run around their coop and bark at them. Ginger has taken to sunbathing and is usually found on his back, legs akimbo in the sunniest spot. He still biffs Shimmer on the nose if she gets too close but they get on pretty well otherwise. Everything is OK as long as Shimmer remembers rule number one: Ginger Is Boss.

Have noted men in suits about the place the last few weeks.

Dad has been in touch with people he calls 'the powers that be' which sounds to me like a sci-fi movie. The Powers That Be: coming soon to a cinema near you.

In reality, they have been here on official business which meant Josh, Shimmer, Ginger and I had to keep out of their way whenever they were here. We can't risk the wee machine (Shimmer) doing anything to upset them.

One lot was to talk about registering our rescue centre as a charity and to get the proper licences for keeping animals in place.

Another lot were The Planners. Not a rock group, they are the men from the council who all seem very serious, shake their heads a lot, look at Mum's architect's drawings and do a lot of pointing. It means things on the Silverbrook Farm project are moving, which is GOOD.

It is also June and the best place to be is on the beach. Caitlin, Shimmer and I head there whenever we can and sometimes we let Robbie come with us too. Caitlin is in heaven because there are boys there, even surfer boys. They think they are mega cool in their shades. The snooty girls hang around a lot, which annoys Caitlin. They walk up and down the beach as though they are on a catwalk, strut, strut,

*turn and flick their hair about a lot as if to say, 'Look
at me, I am soooo gorgeous'. Shimmer is in heaven
because the beach café is open for the summer and it
sells ice cream and sausages.*

*The sun is out, it is Saturday (and I love
Saturdays) and Compton Truit is a happening place
to be. The beach is where I am going now so goodbye
dear diary, adieu.*

I headed for the front door, where I picked up the post
from the mat. I took it into Mum in the kitchen and
she sifted through.

'Richie, there's one here from the council,' she
called out the window to Dad. He came running in as
Mum opened the letter. Her face immediately
dropped. 'Permission refused,' she said.

There was a moment of silence. 'No!' Dad
exclaimed. 'Let me see.' He read the letter and sighed.
'I suppose we can appeal … but it sounds pretty
definite.'

'So back to square one,' said Mum.

'What is it?' I asked.

'The council have refused us permission to convert
the stables and outbuildings,' said Dad.

'But why?' I asked.

'Objections from some of the locals,' said Dad. 'So

they weren't all as on board as we'd thought. And we were all ready to start in a few weeks' time.'

They both looked so fed up. I wished there was something I could do.

'After all our hard work,' said Mum, 'who could have objected?'

Dad shrugged his shoulders. 'I'll try and find out then see what we can do to persuade them round to our way of thinking.' He looked over at me and Shimmer, who was waiting expectantly in the hall with her lead in her mouth. 'You go, Amy; no point in us all hanging around here. I'll make some enquiries and see what we can do.'

'We're still the outsiders, that's what it is,' said Mum. 'No matter what we do.'

Shimmer and I met Caitlin at the end of our lane and we caught the bus to the coast.

'Might be an idea if we take a walk in one of the fields nearby before we head for the beach, that way, Shimmer can let off some steam,' I suggested.

'Yes, we don't want a repeat of the famous wet dog incident,' Caitlin agreed.

When we got off the bus, I kept Shimmer on the lead along the lane but once we reached the open fields to the left of the posh houses, I let her go and she was off, bounding around, sniffing everything in sight with her usual enthusiasm.

I blew my whistle and she came racing back. 'Excellent. Result,' I said.

Caitlin laughed. 'She always looks like she's smiling, doesn't she?'

'That's because she is,' I replied. 'Unlike Mum and Dad when I left them.' I filled her in on the latest news from the council.

'That's just mean,' she said. She opened her arms wide, looked up to the sky and said, 'Dear whoever's up there, we need help down here. We need a miracle … Come on, Amy. Join in. We should do a rain dance to ask the council to change their minds.'

I opened my arms out as Caitlin had done and looked up at the sky. 'Good idea, my mad friend. Anything's worth a go.'

We danced in a circle like Red Indians, put our arms up in the air and Caitlin chanted, 'Ombabumga, good fairies help us. Wicked Witch of the West, release us from your spell. And you too, Snow Queen of Narnia – and whoever else has put a hex on the Silverbrook project.'

I laughed. 'That ought to do it.'

That done, we walked on a bit further and I threw

the ball for Shimmer and off she went. It was so hot that Caitlin and I decided we'd lie on the grass and soak up a bit of sun before heading down to the sea. After a few minutes, I realised Shimmer hadn't come back with the ball. I sat up to look for her and could see her at the far end of the field near a gate. She had her nose to the ground. Clearly, she'd smelled something of interest. I hoped it wasn't a rabbit or a squirrel or someone with a picnic.

'Shimmer!' I called. She looked up then went back to sniffing.

I blew the whistle. She still didn't come back.

'I don't believe it,' I said. 'I really thought she was getting the hang of being obedient.' I got out my little tin of dog treats and shook it. 'Last resort. She always comes when she knows there's something nice for her to eat.'

Shimmer glanced over at us then went back to sniffing. Suddenly, she came bounding over to where we were.

'Good girl,' I said when she reached us and I gave her a treat. 'I shouldn't be having to use titbits at this stage of your training, but never mind.'

Shimmer gulped down her treat then she pulled the end of my jeans with her mouth. 'No, Shimmer,' I said. 'I want to stay here.'

She let go, ran off a few paces then came back and started tugging on my jeans again. She let go and ran off in the direction of the corner of the field and started barking.

'What's she doing?' asked Caitlin.

She was acting really strangely. Running away a short distance, then coming back and tugging at my jeans, then running off again.

'I think she wants us to go with her,' I said. 'No, Shimmer. We want to sunbathe. You run about but not too far.' I lay back down on the grass.

Shimmer woofed and raced off back to the corner of the field, where she began to bark loudly. I sat up.

'I think she's found something,' said Caitlin. 'Let's go and see what she's looking at.'

Reluctantly, we got up and trudged across the field to where Shimmer was busy sniffing the ground.

Caitlin saw him first. A man in the grass wearing rider's gear and a helmet, lying very still. 'Oh my God,' she said and pointed.

It was Mr Pengilly. 'He's been hurt,' I gasped. 'We have to get help, phone an ambulance.'

'I'll do that,' said Caitlin and pulled out her phone.

'And I'll call home,' I said.

Luckily, Mum picked up straight away. 'Mum. We're over at the fields near the beach and Shimmer found Mr Pengilly. I think he might be dead! Caitlin's calling nine-nine-nine, but what if they don't get here in time?'

'Slow down, Amy. Is he breathing?' Mum asked. I could hear the alarm in her voice.

'Caitlin, is he breathing?' I asked.

She leaned over him. 'Yes. I can see his chest moving.'

'Where exactly are you?' asked Mum.

I explained our location. 'I think he might have fallen from his horse.'

'Stay there. Don't move him in case he's hurt his neck. We'll be there as soon as we can. I'll call your dad now. Keep your phone on.'

'Will do.' I clicked my phone shut.

'Mr Pengilly, can you move?' asked Caitlin, but there was no response. She looked at me. 'Do you think we should put him in the recovery position, on his side, like they showed us at school?'

I shook my head. 'Mum said not to move him ... Mr Pengilly, we've sent for help. Try and wake up if you can.'

Caitlin had gone white. 'Amy, I'm scared.'

'We have to stay calm,' I said, though calm was the

last thing I was feeling. 'We don't want to make things worse. Whoa, this is scary. What should we do?'

'I think we should keep talking to him. Remember when we did first aid at school, they said to keep talking to whoever's hurt. We have to try and get him to wake up and he could tell us where he's hurt … Mr Pengilly, Mr *Pengilly*.' She looked at me. 'What do we talk to him about?'

'I don't know. Anything. Er … It's hot isn't it, Mr Pengilly? My dog Shimmer found you. She was sniffing around …' I carried on, talking about nothing, stating the obvious.

It seemed a lifetime that we were waiting, then suddenly Shimmer started barking. We looked over to the other side of the field where we could see a girl on a horse had come into the field.

'I think it's Poppy,' said Caitlin and she stood up and waved.

She came galloping over and slid off her horse. 'Is it my dad?' she asked and when she saw her father, ran over to him and knelt beside him. 'Dad, please wake up!' She started to cry. 'What happened?'

'We don't know. I've called my mum,' I said. 'An ambulance is on its way. He is breathing, Poppy. Don't worry. They'll be here soon.'

Poppy looked like she was going to faint. 'We've

been looking for him everywhere all morning. His horse came back without him. I've been out looking for him for hours.'

'Shimmer found him,' I said.

Poppy took her dad's hand, tears rolling down her face. 'I'm here, Dad, I'm here!'

'Do you want me to call your mum?' asked Caitlin.

Poppy looked even more upset. 'I don't have a mum. She died when I was little. There's only me and Dad.'

I felt so sorry for her. I put my arm around her and Caitlin took her other hand.

'When did you call?' she asked between sobs.

'Twenty minutes ago, they won't be ...' At that moment, I spotted Dad. He came running across the field and knelt beside Mr Pengilly. Moments later, we heard the whir of a helicopter approaching and everything seemed to go into fast forward.

The air ambulance landed on the opposite side of the field and men in green uniforms came running over with a stretcher. In no time, they'd lifted Mr Pengilly on to it as if he was as light as a feather. Dad offered to take Poppy's horse back to her house so that she could go with her father, and then they were gone. The sound of the helicopter grew distant and the field was quiet again.

I noticed Shimmer was sitting at my side, leaning into me and looking at the horse with great suspicion.

I laughed. 'She hasn't seen a horse close up before, or a helicopter,' I said. 'She's probably wondering what kind of creatures they are.'

Dad leaned over and ruffled Shimmer's head. 'Good girl,' he said. 'Good girl.'

Shimmer wagged her tail, but she didn't move. She wasn't going near that horse.

A photo of Shimmer was on the front page of the paper the next day with the headline: *SHIMMER THE WONDER DOG.*

Shimmer, a young golden retriever, was responsible for saving a life yesterday when she alerted her owner that Mr Nicholas Pengilly was in trouble. Pengilly had fallen from his horse along Summer Lane and is in Compton Truit Infirmary, where he is said to be doing well. He said: 'I have to thank Shimmer the dog for finding me, and her owner, Amy Westall, and friend, Caitlin O'Neill, for raising the alarm and staying with me until the air ambulance arrived. I might not have made it if it hadn't been for them.' The Westall family are newcomers to the area and have plans to open a farm shop, café and animal rescue centre. It appears that they rescue people as well as animals!

A letter from the council came a week later. Permissions to build and extend granted. Thank you, God, rain gods and the White Witch of Narnia. Plus Mr Pengilly, who I suspect had something to do with it as well.

Chapter Sixteen

Everybody Loves Shimmer

'Shimmer!'

I'd been having a nice lie-in the morning after our good news, but Shimmer decided it was time for me to get up. Her way of letting me know that was to give my face a lick. Beats an alarm clock I guess. I snuggled down under the duvet in the hope that she'd get the message but she ran over to the door, scrabbled at it, then ran back to my bed and started pulling at the duvet.

'*Shimmer!*' I said again, but she only wagged her tail more once she could see that I was awake.

I got up, pulled on my dressing gown and was just about to go downstairs to give her some breakfast and get some juice when I heard Mum on the phone. She was saying something about

Shimmer. I stopped at the top of the stairs and listened in.

'Oh yes,' she said. 'We've had a lot of enquiries …Yes, she really is the most remarkable dog and such a sweet nature …Yes, a Wonder Dog. Since the article in the paper, there's been a lot of interest in her, but I regret to tell you that we've already found a home for her. Yes. Yes, I will add your name to the list in case they change their minds, but I have to warn you we've already got fifteen names on the list.'

I felt sick as I listened to the rest of the call. Neither Mum nor Dad had mentioned to me that there was a list of fifteen people nor, worst of all, that they'd found a home for Shimmer. When were they planning to tell me? Or were they just going to take her off one day when I was busy doing something else? Did they think I wouldn't notice that my best friend in the world had gone?

I ran back into my room, threw myself on the bed and cried my eyes out. Shimmer came back in to see what was going on, putting her paw up to my face and giving me a lick. That made me cry even more. 'I couldn't imagine life without you, Shim,' I said as I sat up, buried my face in her fur and sobbed some more.

After a short while, there was a knock on my door, then Mum and Dad came in.

'We want to talk to you about Shimmer,' said Dad.

I turned away towards the wall. 'Go away.'

Mum came and sat on the end of the bed. 'Amy, have you been crying? Whatever's the matter?'

I turned back to face them. 'What do you think? I heard you on the phone? *How could you!*'

Dad looked confused. 'How could we what?' he asked.

'I *heard* you, Mum. I heard you say that you've found a home for Shimmer and there's a list of fifteen people waiting for her.' I burst into tears again.

Dad came and sat on my other side. 'Oh Amy, don't cry, baby. We *have* found a home for Shimmer. That's what we came up to tell you. This one! Silverbrook Farm. We couldn't let her go now. She's part of the family.'

I felt like I was in a dream. First such terrible news and now the best news ever. 'Did you just say *this one*? Here? This is her home? Do you mean we're keeping her forever?'

Mum gave me a squeeze. 'Forever,' she said.

Mum and Dad both grinned and Shimmer sensed something was going on. She jumped up on the bed with us and flopped over us, her tail wagging like mad. I gave her a big hug and burst into tears again, but this time through sheer joy. To have thought I might have had to let her go was unbearable – and now I was going to keep her forever. Even Mum and Dad had tears in their eyes.

Chapter Seventeen

The Grand Opening

Dear Diary,
    Today is 20th December and the grand opening
of the Silverbrook Farm shop, café and rescue centre.
Natalia is here! Got to go, things to do, people to
see, a dog, a cat, gerbils, a rabbit and a ferret to feed,
make-up to put on. Deck the halls with Christmas
holly, tra la la la lah, la la la lah.

'Wow, your friend is organised,' said Caitlin as she leaned out of my bedroom window and watched Natalia walk around the yard with her clipboard of lists. Natalia had been down to stay a few times in the summer already, and now she was running around putting all of her Silverbrook plans in motion. I think she'd move in with us if she could.

I laughed. 'Natalia's always been like that. Since we were little. Little Ms Bossy Boots.' I looked up at the sky. 'Hey, look, it's starting to snow.'

Caitlin started singing 'White Christmas' at the top of her voice.

We were up in my room getting ready for the grand opening of the café, farm shop and rescue centre. It was nine in the morning and people would be arriving at two o'clock. Already there were teams of people over in the stable area getting everything ready.

In the last six months, it had felt like someone had pressed the fast forward button on the remote control of our lives. So much had happened. After Mr Pengilly's rescue, the floodgates had opened in terms of local support. Plus Josh's Facebook and Twitter pages had let people know that we were responsible animal carers. The Facebook page already had three thousand likes and the Twitter page had three and a half thousand followers and was growing daily. All sorts of people had come forward offering their skills – painters, decorators, plumbers ... The phone had been busy from morning to night with people wanting either to work or sell their produce. Dad had a good list of people volunteering to act as foster homes for animals until the rescue centre was finished, and already there were two dogs and three cats waiting for their places at Silverbrook Farm. Mrs Carter-West had given Dad a very generous donation to help things along, so hopefully it wouldn't be too long. I'd been for tea at her house a few times with Mum and met her gorgeous cuddly cats, both Persians. They're so funny, like someone squashed their faces flat with a frying pan.

I put some tinsel around Shimmer's collar and we went down to check on the animals in what was the beginning of the rescue centre. The building of the main wing was going to take a few months to complete, but one of the barns opposite the stables had been rebuilt, had a roof put on it and had heating and housing for small animals.

I left Shimmer outside for a minute, lifted the latch on the door and Caitlin and I went in.

'Hi, Albus,' I said to the white ferret, who was bouncing about in his cage. He was only three months old and was so energetic and playful.

Next along was Arthur the grey rabbit. He was very shy so Caitlin and I tiptoed past in case he got anxious and scurried to hide in the corner, as he often did when people were around. 'Dad said in time he'll grow more confident,' I whispered to Caitlin, 'we just have to be patient.'

Caitlin nodded and turned back. 'Hi, Arthur,'

she whispered. 'Hope we can be friends soon.'

Last were Dib and Dob, the ginger-and-white gerbils. As soon as they saw us, they both stood up on their back legs at the front of the cage. 'Hello, cuties,' said Caitlin. 'They're adorable!'

'I know,' I said. 'I wish we could keep them all, but we can't — and someone's coming for Dib and Dob tomorrow. They're going to be someone's Christmas present.'

'Lucky someone,' said Caitlin. 'What about the other two?'

'Josh wants to keep Albus. He's grown very fond of him and I think Mum and Dad might let him as he's only small and is so funny! Dad said that Arthur's not ready to go anywhere yet. He wants him to feel safe first and get used to people. He's small now because he's only four months old, but he will grow very big, into a giant rabbit.'

Caitlin looked shocked. 'Giant? Like proper giant?'

'No, not *totally* enormous, but there is a breed of rabbits that are much bigger than normal ones.'

'Cool,' said Caitlin.

After making sure the little furry ones were OK, we went to join the others in the shop and café, and as we crossed the yard we saw that Dad was busy putting up bunting and fairy lights.

'Isn't the snow great?' I said. 'It will make everything more festive.'

He didn't look as happy about it as I was. 'Hmm,' he said. 'As long as it doesn't stick.'

The farm shop looked fant-ab-ulous, to use Caitlin's phrase. The builders had knocked four of the stables into one and it was now a vast space, with a high ceiling and wooden beams that twinkled with more fairy lights and bowers of ivy and fir. My art teacher, Mrs Rendall, had taken charge of the Christmas decorations and had done a brilliant job using anything she could find in the fields and people's gardens: holly, ivy and whatever else she came across. The room smelled of fresh pine from the massive Christmas tree in the corner. It had been donated by one of the farmers and Mrs Rendall had covered it in hundreds of gold baubles and one wide long ribbon that she'd wound round from the top to the bottom. It looked very classy. Apart from the toy dog we'd insisted go on top instead a fairy. It was a white-gold puppy – and our personal tribute to Shimmer.

The counters were heaving with all the usual farm shop produce: eggs (some from our own hens), meat from local farms, fruit and veg from Mr O'Neill, but also mounds of gorgeous-looking cakes, biscuits, mince pies and puddings.

'Yumbocious,' said Caitlin as she surveyed the displays.

Next door to the shop was the café. The back wall had been knocked out completely and replaced with a huge window, giving a totally amazing view of the countryside beyond. Through it, we could see that the snow had begun to thicken and was sticking to the ground, making it look really pretty, and that was added to by the carols playing over the sound system. It couldn't have looked more festive.

Mrs Watson was already behind the counter making mulled wine, and the scent of oranges, clove and cinnamon filled the air. Mum and Caitlin's mum had Christmas jumpers on – Mum's with a reindeer on the front and Mrs O'Neill's with a penguin. All the staff were wearing Christmas hats, including Liam, and Robbie was dressed as an elf. Even Poppy had made an effort. Since the accident, she'd been much nicer to us and had come up to Silverbrook a few times to help out. She clearly loved animals, especially Shimmer. She was dressed in a gorgeous red velvet dress and was wearing a tiara of red tinsel. She looked as if she'd stepped out of a fairy story – still a princess, but one I was warming to.

Mum pulled out a camera and asked Caitlin, Poppy, Natalia, Shimmer and me to pose in front of the tree.

We put our arms around each other and stood together smiling at the camera. 'The Silverbrook Girls,' said Mum with a grin. I beckoned Robbie, Josh and Liam to come for a photo too. 'Can't leave the boys out,' I said.

'Come and look at the cakes,' said Robbie, after Mum had taken the shot. He pulled me over to the display. He had a smudge of chocolate by his mouth so I suspected that he'd already been helping himself to them. He and Liam had been up to Silverbrook every Saturday since Robbie had taken Shimmer. After a few weeks, Dad had told them that it wasn't necessary and that they'd 'served their time'. But they both kept coming back. Liam said it was because he needed to keep an eye on his brother, but I suspected he liked it here as much as Robbie did. There was to be a prize for the best cake and the villagers had amazed us. The display was mouthwatering – passion fruit, carrot, chocolate logs, Victoria sponges, lemon drizzle, even a yummy-looking Turkish delight cake, as well as the usual Christmas cakes and plates of mince pies.

On another counter there were salads of every variety and plates of sandwiches: egg mayonnaise, coronation chicken, tuna, cheese – enough to feed an army, which was fitting because we were expecting hundreds of people. Natalia had put herself in charge of marketing and got a double-page spread in the local paper, an interview on the radio, as well as posters all over the village and on Josh's Silverbrook Facebook and Twitter pages.

'What time does Tyrrel Turner arrive?' asked Caitlin.

'About one-thirty,' said Natalia. She'd managed to get hold of him through his agent and had written to him telling him about the project. He had phoned and said he'd love to help out in any way he could. That girl really had a flair for making things happen.

'Mum's put a ribbon across the lane and when everyone's ready to come in, he's going to cut it and declare the shop, café and rescue centre officially open,' I added.

Caitlin and I got stuck in helping out where we could and at one o'clock Dad came into the café with a worried look on his face.

'Problem,' he said. 'Mike's just been to the village. The roads are covered in knee-deep snow. He had to abandon his car and walk the last bit.'

Mum's face fell. 'No,' she said. 'No. This can't be happening.'

As news of the roads spread, the mood in the shop changed and the air of excited anticipation was replaced with one of disappointment. What if no one could get here? I felt so frustrated – after all the

179

setbacks we'd been through, we were going to be let down by the flipping weather!

'People could put their wellies on and walk,' I suggested.

Dad shook his head. 'Not the elderly. They won't come out if the roads are hazardous for driving or walking, nor will parents with kids.'

'But we've got Santa's grotto set up in the shop,' I said. It was supposed to be a surprise for the youngest villagers.

'I'm going to call Dad,' said Poppy and got out her mobile.

'I know her dad's a powerful man and all,' said Caitlin in a loud whisper, 'but he can't control the weather.'

Poppy finished her call. 'He'll do what he can,' she said but she didn't look optimistic.

Caitlin looked at me. 'It's that darn Snow Queen of Narnia again,' she said. 'Should we try a snow dance or pray or something? It worked in the summer.'

I grimaced. 'You could try, Caitlin,' I said.

Caitlin squeezed my arm. 'It's not over yet. The snow might turn to rain.'

But for the next hour, the snow continued to fall. It turned one-thirty, one-forty-five and finally two o'clock. A few people had made it up through the snow and reported there were no cars on the road.

'It looks like Siberia out there,' said Liam as he looked outside.

'And how would you know?' asked Caitlin.

'I've seen movies,' said Liam, blushing.

'It looks pretty cold in here too,' I said as I looked around at all the people dressed in their Christmas outfits sitting about waiting for a crowd who weren't coming.

Mrs Watson, Mum and Mrs O'Neill made a huge vat of hot chocolate and all the workers gathered in the café.

The atmosphere was still gloomy.

'Let's sing,' said Caitlin. 'Come on, Christmas carols. Cheer ourselves up a bit.'

No one looked very excited about the idea but she refused to be put off and started singing, '*Deck the halls with boughs of holly* … Come on, everyone!'

Mrs Watson joined in with her.

I looked around at all the sad faces. 'Come on, Robbie, Nat, let's join in.' So we did. Then a few more people began to sing, then a few more, even Liam joined in, and soon the whole café was belting it out.

'Hey, look,' said Liam and he pointed out of the window facing the yard.

Outside was a huge snow dredger and it had cleared the lane up to the stables. Behind the dredger was a procession of vehicles coming up the lane. First a Range Rover with seven people packed in, followed by the school bus full of people – including the snooty girls and surfer boys, next was a pony and trap that was used in the summer to take tourists around and lastly a tractor with a couple of people hanging on. They piled out and into the warmth of the shop.

Mr Pengilly got down from the tractor and went over to Dad. "We've cleared the road best we can and people are heading up. We've also asked the local radio to put out an announcement saying that the road is clear, and there's a whole crowd waiting in the village. A couple more runs of the bus and I reckon we'll have everyone up here.'

Josh got out his phone. 'And I can put it on Twitter,' he said. 'Hopefully a few more people will see the roads have been cleared.'

All was not lost!

An hour later and just about the whole village was up at Silverbrook including our B-list star, Tyrrel Turner. He was surrounded by women of various ages (including Poppy, Caitlin and Natalie). The place was buzzing, the till was ringing, carol singers were singing, kids were outside throwing snowballs, Shimmer was inside trying to steal sandwiches and sausages (of course).

I thought back to when we'd first arrived and I thought Compton Truit was the dreariest place in the universe. I looked around at the festive scene in front of me and saw Tyrrel chatting to Mum whilst the local photographers took photos. Caitlin came over and put her arm around me and gave me a squeeze. 'You've done it,' she said.

I hugged her back. '*We've* done it,' I said as Natalia and Poppy came to join us. 'Team effort. Silverbrook Farm shop, café and rescue centre is really happening.'

Natalia nodded and looked around with satisfaction. 'And this is just the beginning.'

Shimmer ran over to us, tail wagging, and my heart nearly burst with pure happiness. It was hard to imagine that once I'd felt lonely here. As well as Mum, Dad and Josh, now I had Caitlin, Poppy, Robbie and Liam as new friends – plus the furry ones: Shimmer, Ginger, Albus, Arthur, Dib and Dob. I felt a rush of excitement at the thought of what might happen here. Animals would come then go to other homes, but others would replace them. There would be other gerbils, ferrets, rabbits, cats and dogs – and I couldn't wait to meet them and be a part of making their lives safer and happier. 'Today has been good,' I said, 'but the future for Silverbrook Farm looks even better.' I bent over to give Shimmer a stroke. 'Don't worry, Shimmer.

You'll always be our first rescue dog and my bestest furry friend.'

Shimmer put her paws up and gave me her usual response when she approved of something – a big wet lick!

If you liked *A Home for Shimmer*,
try Cathy Hopkins' series for older readers,